F
Ni

Nickolae, Barbara

Finders, keepers

FN

FINDERS
KEEPERS

FINDERS

KEEPERS

Barbara Nickolae

McGRAW-HILL PUBLISHING COMPANY

New York St. Louis San Francisco Bogotá Hamburg
Madrid Mexico Milan Montreal Paris
São Paulo Tokyo Toronto

1 2 3 4 5 6 7 8 9 DOC DOC 8 9 2 1 0 9

ISBN 0-07-046503-7

Library of Congress Cataloging-in-Publication Data

Nickolae, Barbara.
    Finders, keepers / by Barbara Nickolae.
      p. cm.
    ISBN 0-07-046503-7
    I. Title.
  PS3564.I32F5   1989
  813'.54—dc19

                               88-34682
                                 CIP

Book design by Sheree Goodman

To Burt Pronin and John Gerstner

ACKNOWLEDGMENTS

To Gilbert Martin, M.D., for providing information on HLA blood testing, and to Barbara Smith of Salinas, California, for technical assistance.

❦ *Prologue* ❦

HELEN HANSON FELT A SURGE of joy when she reached Monterey Bay.

Glistening like a blue mirror, the water was dotted with boats of every style, color, and size. A few moved gracefully under sail. Others darted along, leaving billowing white trails, and at the shore, sleek yachts shifted gently in their slips. When she was here a week ago, she'd been too upset to realize how breathtakingly beautiful it was, but now she thought it was a picture postcard come to life in the sunlight.

And Neely was here, waiting for her. Thinking of him helped her keep everything else out of mind.

Yesterday, even after she had done exactly what he told her to do, she had been afraid she would never hear from him again. Then last night his assistant called, asking her to come back to the Bay. She took a deep breath. The salt air was soothing. Everything *would* be all right.

She'd loved Neely for years—since they were in high school—and she'd gone to great lengths to follow his career in New York. But daydreams had been her only comfort until a year ago when he returned to California. Determined to see him, she had come up with a plausible reason for getting in touch.

A plausible reason. It had led to the worst mistake of her life.

But Neely had figured a way out and, best of all, he had forgiven her. Helen took another deep breath. Maybe now that she'd proven her devotion, he would care for her.

Eager despite her fears and regrets, she had followed directions carefully. Using a false name, she'd flown to the Bay and taken a cab to within walking distance of the marina. She understood the precautions. He was protecting her, making certain that if she were recognized, she could not be traced.

She ran down the pier, rehearsing one last time what she would say. She had chosen the words carefully. She wanted Neely to know she loved him, would do anything for him—she'd proven that—but she was careful to avoid words with sounds that were difficult for her to say—the kind of words that had caused her so much torment and teasing when she was growing up.

Reaching the *Lorelei II*, she put her arm through the shoulder strap of the small satchel she carried, then grasped the ladder and positioned her foot. She felt awkward swinging her leg over the side to get on board and hoped he wasn't watching.

"Neely?" she called, pleased to use his name in such a proprietary manner. "Neely."

She heard a muffled voice below deck. "Helen, down here."

Taking off her wide-brimmed straw hat, she shook her head to let her hair tumble free. She smoothed her skirt and smiled, trying to look warm and appealing. Then, grasping the thin banister, she walked down the open-backed stairs.

"Helen."

"Neel—" Turning at the sound of her name, she saw a metal pipe descending. She had time for only a moment of surprise.

Her startled expression froze on her face as he delivered the blow. There was a crunching sound, as if a heavy china plate had been slammed into a wall. What was probably meant to be a scream remained little more than a gurgle in her throat. Then everything was quiet, except for the gulls and sounds of the harbor.

He stared down at her. Blood was flowing in a widening circle on the slick, varnished floor. Swiftly, he wrapped her oozing head in towels, but he couldn't take time to mop the floor or clean the splattered walls.

Going up on deck, he looked around. People swarmed the marina, but no one appeared to notice him—and he was sure she had walked to the marina, exactly as he'd told her to do.

He unmoored the *Lorelei II* and headed her out toward open seas. He was a good sailor and had no trouble handling the boat alone. He sailed a distance down the coast, then headed out to sea, where he cast his dead cargo overboard to be carried out by the tide.

This was the second time he had killed, but he assured himself he wasn't a murderer. He was a realist, a man who could do what had to be done. And now he had to clean up the blood.

1

SHANNON BUCHANAN DROVE THROUGH the early morning mist that shrouded the coastline of Monterey Bay, a few miles north of Pacific Grove. She loved the smell of the ocean, the feel of the damp air, but she kept the windows closed, not wanting to chill the little girl who slept curled like a kitten on the back seat.

It was June, but summer comes gently on the rock-strewn coast. In the afternoon, after a few hours of hazy sunshine, the fog would roll in again and weave through the dark pines. The area had a majestic, almost mysterious beauty that fascinated her. From the day they arrived Shannon had felt at home here. She had hoped to stay, to find a place of their own and settle down at last, but now she was on her way to Los Angeles.

Alone, she could have managed, but Mandy needed more of a home than the back seat of a car—and an unreliable car at that. Shannon grimaced, thinking about the hundred dollars she'd spent to get it running again, half of the two-hundred-dollar advance she'd gotten for the job that awaited her. She had promised faithfully to be in Los Angeles that morning, Thursday, but yesterday, just as they were starting the four-hundred-mile drive south, the car had ruptured something or other. She and

Mandy had spent the whole day at the garage, waiting until it was repaired.

She wished Mr. Johnson had given her a telephone number so that she could call him and explain the delay. He'd been very definite about wanting her in his office on Thursday. "I won't be in the office Friday," he'd told her, "and I'll be gone for the weekend, so make sure you're there on Thursday."

Oh well, she'd just have to explain when she saw him. Meantime, there was no point in rushing. She couldn't do any good in L.A. until Monday.

She wished they could spend their last day on the Bay romping on the shore, wading into the cold water and building castles in the sand, but the garage bill had cut deep into her finances.

She shifted to low gear, studying the junction she was approaching. Next to a gas station was a large fruit stand where two farm workers were unloading melons. It was on the main road, and there was enough space for her to set up her easel without getting in anyone's way.

She pulled off the road and parked the old blue Pinto behind the station. Getting out, she stretched, reaching her arms skyward until she felt tall despite her five-foot-three frame. She tucked her T-shirt loosely into her jeans, wanting to look neat but reluctant to accentuate the too-full breasts that didn't match her lean body.

She looked around at the spot she had chosen. No one would stop here just to have her draw a portrait, but she could snag her customers from among the travelers who pulled off for gas or to buy locally grown vegetables and fruits. Humming softly, she took her easel, camp chairs, and display pictures out of the trunk and was all set up before the little girl awakened.

"Shannon, Shannon, where are you?"

Shannon walked back to the car. "Mandy, I'm right here. I found us a good place to work today."

"Me too? Can I say, 'Get a picture made by the real Shannon Buchanan'?"

Her little voice rose in the much-rehearsed singsong of her sales pitch and Shannon laughed. "I couldn't do it without you."

Shannon ran a brush through Mandy's blond curls, then dug through a grocery sack on the floor of the car. "Here's a granola bar. A little later I'll get you an orange juice."

Shannon sat at her easel and Mandy stood by her side, munching her breakfast. They studied the people who pulled into the gas station or stopped to buy produce.

"Him?" Mandy asked, nudging her.

The man she pointed to was pumping gas into his station wagon. The tails of his bright print shirt barely covered his bulging middle. He wore a golfer's cap and had the leisurely air of someone on vacation.

"Mandy, you're getting so good, you can spot them faster than I can. Go get him."

Mandy thrust the empty granola bar wrapper into Shannon's lap, then half skipped, half ran toward the man. Shannon watched, seeing the little girl take a stance with her feet apart, chubby hands on hips, looking up at him.

When Mandy turned and pointed at her, Shannon smiled and waved. The man smiled back, and after he paid for his gas he walked over to her with Mandy tugging his pants leg.

"The little girl tells me you'll draw a picture of me for just two dollars."

Shannon pointed at the pictures on display. "I'll do a chalk portrait of you just like these."

"Only more pretty," Mandy piped.

The man laughed and sat in the camp chair facing Shannon. "I wish I had her on my sales team back in Michigan," he said.

Shannon's smile faded. "Michigan," she repeated. "I used to live in Michigan, but that was a long time ago." She sat pensive for a moment, then shook her head. Flipping open the large drawing pad on the easel, she began to work. The man had full jowls, a small nose, and curly hair. He was easy to do, and she worked quickly.

He liked the finished picture and paid her three dollars for it instead of two. "The extra buck is for the little girl," he said, taking the sketch and heading to his car.

By four in the afternoon, when the meager sunshine gave way to swiftly rolling fog, Shannon was finishing her eleventh portrait, a lighthearted caricature of a balding subject who grinned with delight when he saw it.

"Hey," Shannon yelled, uncrumpling the bills he thrust at her as he headed for his car. "You paid me too much. It's only two dollars. You gave me a five and a one!" She chased after him but, without looking back, he slammed the car door and pulled away.

She looked down at the bills in her hand. "We did one less than a dozen," she told Mandy. "We got a four-dollar bonus and, with our tips, we made more than thirty dollars today."

She squeezed the bills in her hand. "Tonight we'll have a good supper."

The child looked up from her own little drawing pad, her blue eyes wide with mischief, "Good girl, Shannon. Can I have chocolate mouse pie?"

Shannon wiped charcoal from the little girl's cheek and tousled the thick blond curls. "Mandy, you're a trip. Most little girls your age wouldn't even know what chocolate mousse pie is."

The child stood up and thrust her chin forward. "I'm going to be three when I get a birthday."

"It'll be a while before you get your birthday, but my birthday is in August. When it comes, I'll let you blow out all my candles."

"How many candles, Shannon? How many?"

Shannon stretched, arching her back, and reached to pull the constraining rubber band from her honey-colored hair so it tumbled forward to frame her face. "Twenty-three candles, Mandy," she answered, "and I bet you can blow them all out at once."

Shannon looked around. It was chilly now, and the air was damp. "It's getting cold. We'd better load up the car. Then we can go find your pie."

The child put charcoals and pastels into the small compartments of a fishing tackle box while Shannon folded the rickety wood easel and carried it to the car.

"Get in your spot in the back," Shannon said, wrestling with an obstinate door handle.

"You be the driver and I rub your back. You like that, don't you, Shannon?"

"You bet I do. You're my best-ever back rubber. Get in. I'll be right back."

She went back for her camp chair and, as she folded it, she glanced toward the nearly deserted fruit stand. Quickly, without a moment's thought, she snatched up a plastic bag of cherries. She tossed them in the car. "Here, Shanna Anna."

She pulled the car onto the highway and headed south. They would stop for dinner, then drive for a while longer, hopefully getting as far south as San Luis Obispo before stopping for the night.

"Mandy, it's time for a song," Shannon said, glancing back at the child. "What shall we sing?"

"I know. I know. Old Mcdonald had a cherry, eeiieeiioo. One for me and one for Shannon, eeiieeiioo." Mandy popped a cherry in her mouth and handed one to Shannon.

"Be careful you don't swallow a pit," Shannon said.

Mandy sang as loud as she could, more interested in her song than in the cherries. Shannon sang, too, and, leaning forward slightly, she felt Mandy's tiny hands gently stroking her back. She stopped singing long enough to say, "Mmm, Mandy, that feels good."

She started to sing again, making up words that made Mandy squeal with laughter.

They were almost to Carmel when she saw the first flashing red light in her rearview mirror.

She jerked her foot off the accelerator, letting the car slow to fifty-five. But a siren screamed, and then another black-and-white loomed in front of her.

"My God, what's happening? Mandy, get back in your seat."

Shannon hit the brake and, with a lurching motion, drove onto the shoulder of the road. Two more police cars appeared. They were surrounded, and two officers were walking toward the car.

Shannon gasped. One of them had his gun drawn. She'd been stopped before, but they'd never come at her with drawn guns.

The officers looked grim, and one of them said, "Sorry to frighten you, miss, but can we see your license and your registration? And would you mind stepping out of your car?" He leaned down, peering at Mandy in the back seat.

Shannon scrambled for her purse, then got out of the car. "Look, if this is about the cherries, I'm sorry," she said, choking out the words. "I'll pay for them. I didn't think it was such a big deal."

The officer was huge, with white-blond hair. He didn't answer but, looming over her, watched closely as she fumbled for her driver's license and handed it to him.

He looked from the photograph on the license to Shannon. "Is this you, Summer Knight?"

Shannon hesitated. "Yes, sir. That's me."

"This license was issued in Florida, and it expired three months ago."

"I've been traveling, but I'm on my way to Los Angeles. I—I've got a job waiting for me there, and I'll get a California license right away."

Mandy whimpered from the back seat, "Shannon . . . Shannon, I don't like him."

"It's okay, Mandy. Don't be scared. We'll be on our way in a minute."

"Shannon, miss? Did the child say Shannon? I thought you were Summer Knight."

The officer with the drawn gun shifted his position. Shannon blinked. "I am. That is, I was Summer Knight in Florida. I changed my name when I moved."

The officer leaned forward. "Whose child is that, miss? What's her name?"

"Her name is Mandy. She's my daughter. I'm not in any trouble, am I?"

The officer did not answer. Shannon looked around her at the blinking red lights and her fear turned to panic. *Oh, my God. Mandy. It was Mandy. Now. After all this time.*

The officer with the gun came closer, lowering his weapon to his side. He leaned into the car window. "I'll be damned. It is her."

His partner nodded. "The Marsh kid, right?"

"If it isn't, she's a dead ringer."

❧ 2 ❧

As HE HUNG UP THE PHONE Daniel Marsh tried to think, tried to clear his head. At last, light glimmered at the end of the oppressive tunnel that had confined him and Patty ever since Suzy had been kidnapped eleven months ago. He caught his breath. The relentless grief, the helplessness, the torture of watching Patty suffer might soon be over.

A little girl had been discovered near Monterey, within thirty miles of where Suzy had been taken. The police officer who had called said they had reason to believe she might be their child.

Suzy.

Daniel didn't know how to contain himself. It would be an hour before Patty was home from her weekly appointment with her psychotherapist—an hour before he could tell her the news. No— he couldn't wait that long.

He reached for the phone, misdialed, and had to start over. He knew she would sense his joy even before he told her.

"Dr. Wade's office. May I help you?" The receptionist's voice cut through Daniel's euphoria, sounding distant and clinical. It was like the voice he'd heard last summer when he'd telephoned a psychiatrist in Salinas, pleading for help for his wife.

*This is Daniel Marsh, he'd said. I'm calling about my wife, Patricia.
She hasn't eaten anything for almost two days. She just lies on the bed,
clutching a pillow and staring at the wall. I've got to talk to the doctor.
He has to help her.*

They had lived in Salinas only a year, and on the psychiatrist's
recommendation they had moved back to San Diego to be close to
their families and old friends. He got his old job back teaching high
school chemistry. Their relatives had rallied around them, Patty
had continued in therapy, and she was better now. A long way
from normal, but better.

Abruptly, Daniel realized that if this wonderful news was all a
mistake—if she got her hopes up and the child wasn't Suzy . . .

"Dr. Wade's office," the receptionist repeated. "Is anyone on
the line?"

Quietly, as if she could identify him if he made a noise, Daniel
hung up the phone. Better to tell Patty face to face when she came
home.

He looked out the kitchen window into their enclosed backyard.
Danny Joe was riding his tricycle up and down the narrow patio
and border of concrete they'd recently put in for that purpose. It
was the only place the boy was allowed to ride. Patty became frantic
at the thought of his riding in front of the house, even with one of
them watching him.

Apart from his own grief over Suzy, Daniel had to witness
Patty's pain. He was unable to protect her, and that was the one
thing he'd wanted to do from the first time he ever saw her.

He was a high school chemistry teacher, tall ana awkward and
shy around women—but he had never felt shy with Patty. He'd
first seen her standing in the corridor between their two classrooms.
Single, she taught a class in marriage and the family. Her light
brown hair was pulled tight in a bun, and she wore glasses with
enormous frames. She was slightly plump and very prim, but somehow she put him at ease. Beneath her primness, he sensed a loving
nature. Before he'd known her a week, he realized he had to marry
her. That was the only way he could take care of her.

Danny Joe dragged his tricycle on the patio. "Daddy," he called, "can I ride out in front? Just for a little while, just until Mommy comes home?"

Daniel opened the sliding glass door. "I don't think so, sport," he said, lifting his son and hoisting him into the air. "Mommy likes it better when you play back here, and anyway it's time for your bath."

He carried the boy inside, roughhousing with him for a few minutes until it was time to bathe him and put him to bed. Danny Joe had light hair like Patty's, but the square jaw and wide-set eyes were a mirror image of Daniel's own.

Suzanne had been born when Danny Joe was two, completing the perfect family. Daniel had the sweetest, most caring wife, the best son, the most adorable little girl.

He and Patty loved the northern part of the state, and when he was offered the job of assistant principal in a high school in Monterey County, they'd both been delighted. He had moved his family north and into a new home—a standard, three-bedroom house they'd loved even though it looked like all the others on the block. Daniel had enjoyed making improvements, but since they'd moved back to San Diego he never worked around the house. Things like wallpaper and new shelves didn't matter anymore.

He paced the room, then flicked on the television. He stared toward it, unseeing.

How many times had he sat at Patty's side, staring at a television neither of them saw? Patty rarely talked, but when she did she picked the same thread, the same train of thought. Daniel knew that in her head she went over that day again and again and again:

"I had bought Suzy new shoes, and we were on our way home, but I needed to stop in the ladies' room. I was going to take Suzanne into the stall with me, but the stroller wouldn't fit and I was struggling with my packages. This woman put her packages on the lounge and said she would watch her for me. I didn't think anything of it. I would have done the same thing myself. I was only in the stall for a minute—really, Daniel, only a minute. When I stepped out, the stroller was empty. Suzanne and the woman were gone. . . ."

Her voice would rise until it was edged with hysteria. "Do you think the woman is taking good care of her, Daniel? Do you?"

Daniel would stroke her arm, trying desperately to comfort her, knowing there was nothing he could do to ease her pain.

Patty had undergone hypnosis to help her recall more about the woman's appearance, and Daniel had stayed with her every minute. "Plain. Not very tall," Patty had said. "Long blond hair, thick bangs. Funny hair, like a wig. Big sunglasses. Pants, a white blouse. She's holding packages. Her voice is funny. Nasal. As if she has a cold. I can hardly understand her."

The woman's packages had proved to be a ruse—large bags with the store's imprint but stuffed with newspapers and old rags. The newspapers had been local, no leads there; no unidentified fingerprints on the stroller. It was obvious the woman had planned the kidnapping. She'd been in the ladies' room waiting for the right woman with the right child, and his sweet, loving Patty had entrusted her with little Suzy.

After the first, nightmarish week, there had been nothing to do but wait. Every knock at the door, every ring of the phone set them tense with fear and hope.

Now, finally, a call had come. Maybe it was better that Patty hadn't been home. He needed time to prepare himself, to get himself under control, so that he could help her face the possibility of disappointment.

When he heard her pull into the driveway, he turned off the television and opened the door, trying to affect the boyish grin he knew she liked. She got out of the car and, without glancing toward him, she moved Danny's tricycle to its assigned place between the dusty golf clubs and the far wall of the garage. She picked up the red plastic laundry basket from where he'd left it on top of the washer and hung it on a peg.

Her precision—her need to have everything exactly in its place—was a symptom that broke Daniel's heart.

She was slimmer now, but she took no pleasure in her petite figure. She took no pleasure in anything. Before entering the house she stared up and down the street, looking, always looking.

Finally, coming into the house, she gave him a distracted kiss.

"Hi," he said, struggling to sound casual, "how was your session with Dr. Wade?"

"Fine. Where's Danny Joe?"

"He played in the backyard for a while, then I gave him a bath and put him to bed."

He took her hand. "Patty, let's sit down. I have to talk to you."

He'd kept his voice casual, but leading her into the family room, he felt her hand tense. He pulled her down to sit beside him on the old blue sofa.

"About an hour ago I had a phone call."

"Suzanne," she said. "It's Suzanne."

"There's a chance—just a chance—they may have found her. There's a little girl up north—not far from where we used to live. She's the right age, and she was found with a transient."

Patty gasped for breath, and Daniel stroked her arm. "They have reason to believe it may be our Suzy. They want us to come and have a look."

"Is she all right?"

"The little girl is fine. The officer said she seems normal and healthy and that she's a real chatterbox."

Patty folded her hands as if in prayer, talking and crying at the same time. "It's Suzy. I know it. Thank God, I'm going to get my baby back. I'll make everything up to her. Everything. And I'll make it up to you, too, Daniel—for what you've suffered."

Daniel chose his words carefully, his uneasiness mounting. "Patty, please. It's too soon to know for sure. The woman she was found with claims to be her mother. For all we know, she is."

Patty stopped crying and stared at him, her eyes wide. "Tell me . . . tell me exactly what the officer said."

"He said they had reason to believe it was Suzy."

Patty jumped up. "Of course it's Suzanne! He wouldn't have

called unless they were sure. Where is she? We have to go to her now!"

"They're holding her in Salinas."

"We'll fly up tonight."

"Patty, I want you to realize—" He couldn't get her to listen.

"Call the airport. Hurry," she insisted. "Then phone your mother to come and stay with Danny Joe. I'll pack clothes for Suzanne. No! Her clothes will be too small for her now. That's all right. I'll buy her new ones tomorrow. Hurry, Daniel, hurry."

He caught her arm. "Please, honey, slow down. We'd better take it easy until we know for sure."

She shook him off. "Daniel, I *am* sure! Make the reservation. Phone your mother. I'll get my things."

She rushed toward the bedroom. "Suzy, Suzy, we're on our way. Mommy and Daddy are coming."

Daniel rose and moved toward the phone. "Please, God, don't let her be disappointed. Let it be Suzy. Please, God."

❧ 3 ❧

IT WAS NEARLY FIVE, only half an hour until the end of Phil Tewkes' shift, when they brought the woman and the child into the Monterey County sheriff's station in Salinas. He had intended to spend the evening at home—maybe a pizza from Jake's, a beer or two, and three or four hours of concentrated work on his newest model, a replica of the Venezuelan clipper ship *Simón Bolívar*.

But he was the only investigator available, and when he took the call from the intake officer, he groaned inwardly. *Suspected kidnapping*. He knew if he began an interrogation now, he might be tied up for hours. They could keep the woman waiting overnight of course, but something had to be done about the child.

Kicking himself, he agreed to look over Deputy Vaughn's preliminary notes. Might as well live up to his reputation—a soft touch when there was extra work to do. At thirty-six Phil was tall and slender. He had a pleasant if somewhat forgettable face, his hair and pale complexion a subtle reminder of the red-haired and freckle-faced kid he had been, and a relaxed gait and unassuming manner that some mistook for indifference. He'd never thought of himself as good-looking—but he'd never much cared.

Now, rising deliberately if without enthusiasm, he ambled out to the desk. He saw the suspect, a young blond woman, hugging the child protectively as the intake officer tagged her belongings. He scanned Vaughn's notes, then watched the social worker struggle to take the child. Both crying, the young woman and the child clung to each other even tighter.

Phil walked over. "You're making it harder on the child," he said softly. "Let her go, and I promise we'll take good care of her."

Looking up at him, the woman released her grasp on the little girl. "It's okay, Mandy. It . . . it won't be long."

"Sue." Phil nodded to a waiting deputy, signaling his intention to get started.

Still sniffling, the woman allowed herself to be led into an interrogation room, though she strained backward to see where the child was being taken. Once inside, she thrust her chin forward and sat stiffly in a chair.

She wasn't bad-looking, Phil decided, studying her from across the room. Too skinny maybe, dressed in worn jeans and a pink T-shirt smudged with color. And she was scared, wide-eyed like a cornered doe, watching him.

Phil didn't speak. He'd learned long ago in interrogations to wait and let the suspect speak first. Sometimes the first words out of a suspect's mouth told him more than hours of questioning.

But the woman said nothing, only watched him with her large, frightened eyes as Sue Ramos took an unobtrusive seat near the back of the small room.

"What's that stuff on your shirt?" he asked, circling her chair slowly.

"Chalk," she said. "Where is that woman taking Mandy?"

"Mandy? Is that her name?"

"Amanda Desiree. Where is she?"

"She'll be just fine. Don't you worry about her. Chalk, you said? What kind of chalk?"

"Pastels." She brushed impatiently at her shirt. "I draw chalk portraits for a living."

"No kidding." Phil nodded, lifting his brows. "An artist. Is that what you are?"

She smiled, surprising him, and looking then more like a girl than a woman. "Yes, an artist. A portrait artist. I make enough money to support myself and take good care of my Mandy."

Phil nodded again, keeping his pace slow. "What did you say your name was?"

A hesitation. "It's Shannon—Shannon Buchanan. I told the other officer that. My name is Shannon Buchanan."

"Shannon Buchanan. Pretty name . . . so is Summer Knight."

"Yes, well, you mean the name on my driver's license. I got that license when I was living in Florida. I was young then. I liked the sound of Summer Knight and that's how I signed my pictures."

"I see," Phil said. "Are there any other AKA's we should know about? Any other names you liked the sound of?"

"No," she said, too emphatically. She was lying, but he let it go.

"Where do you live?"

Again, a hesitation. "We came to Pacific Grove hoping to settle here, but now we're on our way to Los Angeles."

"So you told the other deputies, but where did you come from? What's your address?"

Shannon, if that was her name, looked confused. "Well, I don't exactly have an address. Since we left Texas we've been traveling, and sort of"—she paused—"living in the car."

Her voice rose. "But I've been promised a good job in Los Angeles, and as soon as I can I'm going to find us a real place with a bathtub and a nice bed for Mandy."

"I see," he said. "You and Amanda Desiree. What's Amanda's last name?"

"Knight. Amanda Desiree Knight."

"Knight. Is that her father's name? Where is he?"

She bit her lip. "In Florida, I think. At least that's where he was the last time I saw him. But his name doesn't matter. He doesn't know about Mandy. He doesn't know she was ever born."

"How old is Mandy?"

She answered immediately. "She's nearly three. Her birthday is October 29."

"Where was she born?"

"In Arkansas."

"Where in Arkansas?"

"In . . . well, I don't remember the name of the town."

"You don't remember? Were you living there?"

"No, not exactly. Why are you asking me all these questions?"

She had a childish innocence, a guilelessness he found refreshing. But she was hiding something, and he knew it was time to show impatience. "Buchanan, do you have Mandy's birth certificate? Any proof that you're really her mother?"

She jerked to her feet. "Of course I'm her mother! Why would you ask me that? I haven't done anything. You have no right to keep us. I want my little girl."

"If she really is your little girl, of course you'll get her back. You've been read your rights. I have to tell you—you're under suspicion of kidnapping."

A range of expressions crossed her face. She fell back into her chair. "No." She shook her head. "No, that's not right. You can't kidnap your own child."

He studied her carefully, closing in, his voice barely above a whisper. "*Is* she your child? Or did you take her from a Salinas department store eleven months ago?"

"A Salinas department store? Eleven months ago?" Smiling, she pushed back her chair and stood up. "You have me mixed up with somebody else. I don't even know where Salinas is."

Phil watched her thrust out her chin. In defiance? Indignation? Either she was telling the truth or she was a better actress than he took her for. "Easy," he said. "If you're telling the truth, we'll straighten this all out quickly. I need to know where Mandy was born. We'll have to check it out."

The moment he mentioned Mandy's birthplace, her show of confidence deserted her. She dropped back into her chair. Was she telling the truth or wasn't she?

She struggled. He could see it in her face and the way she twisted in her chair. Why was she so reluctant to say where the birth had taken place?

She searched for words that wouldn't come. She opened her mouth as though to speak, but instead her face crumbled and she burst into tears.

Phil stared at her, frustrated, then threw up his hands and began to pace the room. Deputy Ramos took a tissue from a box on the table and handed it to Shannon.

Still pacing, Phil shook his head, glancing at her now and then. Something was the matter with the whole fabric of what she was telling him. She seemed adamant when she insisted the child was her daughter, yet she had to be lying when she said she couldn't remember the name of the town where she was born.

"How much did Mandy weigh at birth?" he shot at her.

"Six pounds, seven ounces, and she was nineteen inches long. She was beautiful. Really. From the first day, she was as pretty as could be." Tears still rolled down her cheeks, but the hint of a smile brightened her face, as if remembering could please her even now, under these circumstances.

Puzzled, Phil pushed harder. "You can remember her birth weight but not the name of the town where the birth took place. Is that what you're trying to sell?"

She started squirming again. "Listen, I'm not trying to sell you anything. Mandy is my daughter. I take very good care of her, and no one has the right to take her away from me."

"Let me ask you something. Why did you think you were being pulled over when the deputies stopped you?"

"I didn't know. I thought . . . well, I thought it was because I had picked up a bag of cherries and sort of forgot to pay for them."

"You thought four cars stopped you because of some cherries?" His voice was deliberately harsh. "You wouldn't see that much action if you uprooted the whole tree. No, Buchanan, you were pulled over on suspicion of kidnapping. If that's your kid, you'd better try to remember where she was born."

She was breathing hard and her knuckles were white from grasping the sides of her chair. He let her stew for a few minutes while he reviewed what he knew.

The girl was a transient, living out of a car, drawing pictures to feed herself and the kid. He looked down at the list of her belongings the intake officer had handed him. She'd been carrying a little over two hundred dollars—a one-hundred-dollar bill and the rest in ones and fives.

He cut through her distress to ask her about it. "Where did you get the hundred-dollar bill?"

She didn't look up. "I met a man—his name is James Johnson—who wants me to do some real portraits for him in Los Angeles. In oils. He gave me two hundred dollars as an advance, so I could buy canvas and supplies." She sniffled. "I was supposed to meet him in Los Angeles today, but yesterday my car broke down. It took all day to get it fixed, and it cost me ninety-six dollars."

He was about to ask her how he could reach James Johnson when someone tapped at the door. Annoyed, he opened it a crack.

"Sorry to interrupt," the desk officer said, "but I thought you'd want to know. Daniel Marsh just called from the San Diego airport. They'll arrive in Monterey in less than two hours. I told him we'd pick them up and bring them here."

"Daniel Marsh!" Phil barked. "Who the hell called the Marshes?"

The young deputy backed away. "Vaughn, I guess. He made the pinch."

Phil slammed the door shut with sufficient force to make Shannon jump. "Look," he said, jamming both hands in his pockets, "I think we've talked enough for now. I'm going to suggest that Deputy Ramos get you some dinner. While you eat it see if your memory improves. I'd like to help you if Mandy is your kid, but when we talk again I want straight answers."

He walked around the table to stand beside her chair. "First and foremost—where was Mandy born? The town, the hospital, the doctor."

He turned and charged out of the room, looking for Vaughn. When he found him the young deputy's towering frame was hunched over an IBM Selectric. His white-blond hair was carefully styled; he looked as sharp as the crease in his pants—everybody's movie version of a cop. "Who instructed you to call the Marshes?"

Vaughn's attention remained riveted on the typewriter. He shook his head and held up an index finger, but Phil was not about to wait. He hit the power switch, turning off the typewriter. "Now, Vaughn. Talk to me now. Who the hell told you to phone the Marshes?"

"No one. This is my pinch. I recognized the suspect from an APB, and I'm the one who brought her in. And did you see the kid? Look at this and tell me it's not the Marsh girl." He flipped a photo across the desk and sat back, grinning.

As Phil studied the photo his annoyance ebbed. Even considering that the child called Mandy was a good deal older than the Marsh baby was when this picture was shot, the resemblance was unmistakable. Nonetheless, Vaughn had gone off half-cocked when he notified the Marshes. "Who filed the APB?"

"The Highway Patrol—it was on the wire. Any decent cop—"

"Just tell me who filed the information." Phil's voice left no room for theatrics.

"Some guy called the Highway Patrol in Santa Barbara—told them that he had just seen the Marsh kid's picture on a poster—that this woman had the kid and was on her way to L.A."

"And that was enough to send you rolling out with a backup of three more black-and-whites? Listen, hotshot—" Phil was ready to nail Vaughn to the wall, but as he spoke he became aware of a small commotion behind him.

Howie Simms, a photographer from the local daily, led a contingent of reporters. "Howdy, Phil," Simms drawled. "Hear you've got a big one by the tail."

Phil stared. "What's that supposed to mean?"

Howie grinned. "Don't be coy. Word is you've got the Marsh kid—that kid who was kidnapped last year in Salinas."

"What the . . . where did you get your information?" As he spoke he glared at Vaughn.

Vaughn looked puzzled. "Not me. Hey, Tewkes, how stupid do you think I am?"

Phil would have loved nothing better than to tell him, but this wasn't the time or the place—not with more of the press crowding in and the Marshes on their way. If he didn't buy off the reporters before the Marshes arrived, the place would turn into a circus.

"Listen, guys," he said smoothly, "I think someone has jumped the gun here." But even as he spoke he knew it was too late. He wished he'd gone home to work on the *Bolívar*.

❧ 4 ❧

SHANNON HAD NEVER FELT so alone and afraid, and not just because she was in a jail cell. There was so much she could not tell them. But one thing was certain. She loved Mandy and had to get her back.

She sat back on one corner of the bunk, her arms resting on her knees, and watched the last slanting rays of the sun fade from the rough concrete wall.

A tray of food lay beside her on the bunk, spaghetti congealing in a reddish brown sauce and a huge chunk of watermelon. The spaghetti was impossible. She tried to eat the melon but gagged on the second bite, though she had always loved watermelon. As a child she had never gotten enough of it.

But then in Michigan she'd never gotten enough of anything—not food, not understanding, not love. Not even notice. It wouldn't surprise her now to know her parents never noticed she was gone.

She had just graduated from high school when she decided there was nothing to keep her in Michigan. She'd boarded a bus with a gym bag full of her clothes, chalks and drawing pads, and nearly one hundred dollars in baby-sitting money.

She chose Daytona Beach because she liked the sound of it—

exotic and full of promise. Her money took her only as far as Atlanta, but that was okay with her. She was more than two-thirds of the way to Daytona Beach, and she would earn enough money to get there.

Atlanta was bigger and busier than she'd expected, but she'd found a job in a pizza house almost at once.

She had started by hostessing, but one rainy Sunday, when the crowd was small, she hauled out her drawing pad and began sketching caricatures of some of the regular patrons. They were delighted, and so was Mr. Bianco, the owner, who quickly saw her talent as a boon to his business. Before long the place was nearly always full, and her share of the extra money from delighted patrons mounted up quickly.

It took her three months to earn what she needed. She had just celebrated her nineteenth birthday when she boarded the bus for Daytona Beach.

The ocean was a revelation to her—the mild weather, the salt breeze making poetry of the palm trees as she sketched them. She loved Daytona Beach from the first day. It was there on the sand, during one particularly beautiful sunset, that she took the name Summer Knight.

The beach was crowded with tanned, handsome young men, most of them on vacation from college, armed with the most ingenious ploys for trying to get her into bed.

Trevor was different. He sat close to her for days, watching her sketch, seeming content just to be near her. He worried when he found out she had no real home, that the room she rented on a weekly basis was cramped and tiny and humid.

Summer, as she called herself then, insisted it was all she needed because she spent most of her time on the beach. But she was touched by his concern. They enjoyed each other's company, and it was easy, on those balmy summer evenings, for affection to turn to something more.

He talked about taking her home to meet his family, and she daydreamed about a home of their own and what it would be like to be married. Then she learned she was going to have his baby, and she hoped Trevor would be as thrilled as she was.

He was not. He wanted to finish school, and abortions were easy at the clinic, he told her. She'd cringed, knowing for sure she didn't want an abortion. One week later she left Florida.

Shannon sighed, remembering Summer as if she had been another person.

She pushed the tray away. It was getting late, and Mandy would be frightened. She hoped they were taking good care of her.

Daniel Marsh had known the police would be waiting for them at the Monterey airport, but he hadn't expected all the reporters and the blinding glare of flashbulbs. He put his arm around his wife, guiding her to the waiting police car, shielding her as much as he could.

Patty seemed oblivious. She stared straight ahead, almost holding her breath, and again in the car he tried to prepare her in case the child was not Suzanne. "I'm praying it's Suzanne, I'm praying it is. But if it isn't, well . . . if it isn't, it still shows that the police are looking for her. That someday we'll get her back."

Patty turned her face toward his. She smiled and light shone in her eyes. "It *is* Suzanne. We've been waiting all this time, and now we're almost together again."

"Patty, what if it isn't Suzanne? We've got to be ready for that."

Still smiling, she patted his hand. His warning hadn't fazed her. He slumped back, trying hard to hold nothing but hope in his heart. He tightened his grip on her as the black-and-white pulled up in front of the station.

A microphone was thrust inside the car. "Do you believe the child the police have is your daughter?"

"How do you feel about the woman who kidnapped her?"

"What were you doing when you got the news?"

A tall, blond officer muscled everyone aside and led them into the back of a large, imposing building. "I'm Deputy Vaughn," he began. "The substation is down here, in the basement of the court-house, and—"

Patty didn't let him finish. "Is this where my baby is?" she demanded.

A reporter tagged at their heels. "Mrs. Marsh, do you think you'll recognize her after all this time?"

Patty stopped and stared at the man. "I'll know my Suzy. I'll know her."

A young female officer escorted them down a hall, stopping outside a closed door. Daniel Marsh's breath froze in his chest. After a moment that seemed to stretch out forever, the officer swung the door open.

The child looked up from her crayons and papers. "Shannon?" The smile that lit her face was fleeting. "You're not my Shannon. Where is she?" Her chin quivered, and she looked at the gray-haired woman next to her, as if for reassurance.

Daniel knelt at the child's side, brushing away the tears and smoothing the mop of yellow-gold ringlets away from her perspiring face. "Suzy?" His voice was tentative.

At the sound of Patty's sharp intake of breath, he turned. She was rigid, staring. He could feel the tunnel closing in. He could not let it happen. He picked up the child and carried her to Patty. "Honey, look, it's our Suzy."

Wordlessly, Patty took the child and held her close. The little girl squirmed. Then a loud scuffling sounded outside the window. Footsteps. "It's her," a voice outside shouted. "Bring the Minicam! It's her!"

The door burst open. "Who let reporters in here?" A commanding figure spoke.

The woman officer who had escorted them down the hall moved quickly to his side. "Sorry, Phil. They weren't in here. Some damn fool was spying through the window."

"You're Mr. Marsh?" the man said, looking at Daniel. "I'm sorry. This should have been a private moment. My name is Tewkes, Investigator Phil Tewkes." He smiled wryly. "I'm supposed to be in charge. I'd like to move you down the hall to my office. We can be alone in there. . . . Mrs. Forbes," he said to the gray-haired woman, "you can wait for us here if you like."

At the opening of the door, reporters rushed forward, but Tewkes effectively blocked their path and herded the three of them, the child in Patty's arms, to an office farther down the hall.

Iris Forbes did not like crowds, and the doorway was jammed with people. She would have preferred to slip away quietly and wait for the child to be returned to her for placement in temporary foster care. But the reporters wouldn't let her leave. Microphones were thrust within an inch of her face. She found herself badgered with questions:

"Can you tell us what went on in there?"

"Do the Marshes think she's their daughter?"

"What's your name?"

"I . . . I'm Iris Forbes," she began hesitantly. "I'm a social worker for Monterey County." She ran a hand distractedly through her hair. Suddenly, she wished she'd had it styled.

"Mrs. Forbes, did the little girl seem to recognize her parents?"

Iris cleared her throat. "No, she didn't recognize them, but she's very tired right now."

"Is there any doubt about the kid being Suzanne Marsh?"

"That's for the police to say. But in my opinion," she said, warming to the microphone, "she gave no indication that the woman she was found with was her mother."

"Does the woman claim to be her mother?"

"I've never seen her, but I've been told that yes, she is claiming that the child is her daughter."

"What do you think?"

Iris could hear the hum of the cameras. They were trained on her, and people were writing down every word she said. She thought very carefully before she spoke. "She is a very precocious child, very verbal. When I interviewed her I detected one unusual behavior pattern almost immediately. She didn't ask for her mommy. She asked for her Shannon."

"Does the child respond to the name Suzanne?"

"She's clearly confused about her name. First, she said it was Mandy, but when I asked her if she had any other names, she responded with several. I believe the name Shanna Anna was one of them. I'd have to consult my notes for the others."

Phil Tewkes barged into their midst. "What the hell is going on here? We're carrying on an investigation. It's too early to make statements to the press." He glared meaningfully at Iris Forbes.

"Come on, Phil. This is news and you know it. We've already talked to Vaughn."

"Vaughn is not conducting this investigation. When I have a statement to make, you'll hear it."

"Listen, Phil, there doesn't seem to be much doubt in anybody's mind that this is the Marsh kid."

"That's an assumption on your part." He started to walk away, dragging Iris Forbes with him, when the desk sergeant hailed him. "Hey, Phil, you've got a call on line two."

Phil cursed under his breath. "Do me a favor and clear out, all of you. I promise to have a statement within the hour." It would do no good, but he had stated his position. He moved to pick up the phone.

"Phil? Roger Connelly. I hear you have your hands full."

"Yeah, I guess you could say that." Phil respected the district attorney. He was bright, sincere, and dedicated. But he, too, Phil suspected, had been alerted too soon. There was nothing yet to report.

Connelly went on. "Friend of mine tells me you've recovered a missing child. Congratulations. Good work. I'm going to issue a formal statement congratulating you in public. I can imagine how the Marsh parents must feel."

"I don't want to jump the gun, Roger," Phil said, surprised at the feeling in Connelly's voice.

Connelly chuckled. "You've always been conservative, Phil. Nothing wrong with blowing your own horn. But go over what you've got with Lawler and let him make the decision."

"Right," Phil said. "I appreciate your interest. But I don't want to be precipitous—"

"Tewkes!" Ramos called. "You gotta get these reporters out of here! The Marshes want to take the kid home!"

"Listen, Roger. I have to go. But do me a favor, will you? Don't go making any public statements till I tell you I know we've got a case."

Roger sounded coolly professional. "On the other hand, don't go overboard. After all, from what I hear, the child was found with a transient. If she can't substantiate her claim to the child and the parents of the missing child can identify her, go ahead and send her home."

"You know me, Roger. One thing at a time. I'll keep you advised through Lawler." Phil hung up and hurried down the hall toward the commotion.

He surveyed the pandemonium in the hallway. "Listen, guys, give these people a break. They deserve a little privacy. You can wait outside, and you'll see them when they leave. Come on, get out of my way."

Grumbling, the reporters and photographers filed out. Phil continued down the hall. He opened the door to his private office and felt strangely like an intruder.

The child was asleep in Daniel Marsh's arms, her damp, blond head resting on his shoulder. Marsh's other arm was around his wife. They had not heard him come in. He watched for a moment as Patty Marsh reached up to stroke the child's arm. Phil backed out and quietly closed the door. *What in hell should he do now?*

He couldn't jerk the child out of their arms. Obviously, they accepted her as their own. Maybe Connelly was right. Once they identified her, what more proof did he need? But he found himself walking decisively to the holding cells at the end of the hall.

He felt like Solomon. Which of these mothers would settle for half a child? There was no way to know until, like Solomon, he backed them against a wall.

❧ 5 ❧

THE WOMAN WHO CALLED HERSELF Shannon Buchanan rose from her bunk as Phil approached. "Are you going to let me out?" She grasped the bars of the cell. "When can I see Mandy?"

"When you give me some answers that make sense." Phil picked up a straight-backed chair, hauled it over in front of the cell, and straddled it backward to face her.

She looked wary. "What do you want to know?"

"Your name, for openers. And I don't mean Shannon. Or Summer Knight either, for that matter. I mean the name you were born with. And don't tell me you can't remember."

"Valeria Valentine."

"Oh, shit!"

"Okay . . . it's Ruth Ann Stone."

Phil considered. "Ruth Ann Stone. Where were you born, Ruth Ann Stone?"

"I was born in Michigan—honest, in Michigan! But I'm not Ruth Ann anymore. I'm called Shannon—Shannon Buchanan, and what difference does it make where I was born?"

"What makes a difference is where you came from and how long you've been in California."

"I told you," Shannon wailed. "We were traveling cross-country—me and Mandy. I wanted to settle in Pacific Grove. But I haven't been making very much money, and when Mr. Johnson—I told you about him—when he offered me the chance at a job in L.A., well, we decided to go."

"You told me earlier you'd never been in Salinas. Weren't you here eleven months ago?"

"No. I've never been here before—not until I decided to come to Pacific Grove."

"And Mandy. You told me she was born in Arkansas. What were you doing in Arkansas?"

"Just—stopping. To rest. I was out to here." She moved back from the bars to extend her arms and show him how big she'd been in pregnancy.

She smiled as though she expected a response, but Phil kept his face stony. "I want to know the name of the town—the town where Mandy was born. If she was born to you, as you say she was, there'll be a birth certificate on file."

The girl turned and walked the length of the cell, her hands clenched into fists. "I—please," she said. "Why do you have to know? Why are you hounding me?"

"I'm not hounding you. You're avoiding answers. Where was Mandy born?"

"I—can't—there's a reason, really there is. Why can't you just believe me?"

Phil's voice took on an ominous tone. "Because, Ruth Ann Stone, there's a couple down the hall who believe Mandy is their child. That her name is Marsh. Suzanne Marsh, who was abducted seventeen miles from here in Salinas—and you could fit the description of the kidnapper. Unless you can prove you gave birth to that child, she is going home with them."

The woman's face blanched, her translucent skin becoming a ghastly white. "N-no," she whispered. "No, that's not true."

Phil rose from his chair, scraping it back across the floor, the sound echoing in his ear. He'd had enough of this whimpering woman. He began to stride back up the hall. He had one hand on the outer door when he heard her piteous wail.

"Wait!" she cried, banging on the bars. "Wait! Come back! I'll tell you!"

And he knew, as he turned and slowly walked back to her, that this time he would get the truth.

It was nearly midnight and Phil was bone weary when he walked slowly back to his office. He would order a computer check on Ruth Ann Stone, Summer Knight, and Shannon Buchanan—but he couldn't check out the details of her child's alleged birth until morning.

If he had to play Solomon, he wished he had more to go on. Earlier he'd read the computer printout on the Marsh kidnapping, but there'd been nothing in it to help him. The abducted child had no identifying birth marks or scars and was too young to have had dental records or much of a medical history. She had blond curly hair, blue eyes, and was chubby. A unique description, Phil reflected. It could fit only a million kids.

Standing in the corridor, he considered his options—and the time. He could assign the child to Mrs. Forbes and have her put in shelter care for the night. Or he could let the Marshes take her—but he couldn't let them take her very far.

His hand paused on the doorknob. It had been late when the Marshes arrived. The child had been sleepy, the parents over-wrought. Could they have made a mistake? Maybe, if they'd been too hasty, and he allowed them to keep her overnight, there was a chance they'd realize it themselves.

He swung the door open. Marsh still held the sleeping child, his wife sitting quietly beside them. They looked exhausted, but as Phil entered Marsh glanced up sharply. "We are ready to take our daughter home," he announced in a calm voice.

"I wish I could be as sure as you are that she is your daughter. But I won't be until I check out some things, and we can't do that until morning."

Marsh started to protest and his wife frowned anxiously, but Phil went on. "I'll let you take her, but only to a local motel. I need you to stay in the area. We'll call ahead to the motel, then drive you over in an unmarked car."

"I understand, and of course Patty and I will stay in the area tonight. I can't tell you how much we appreciate everything you're doing."

Mrs. Marsh looked up for the first time. "Danny Joe," she murmured. "We'll have to call your mother to find out how he is and let her know we won't be home until tomorrow."

Phil only half heard Marsh's reply. His hand was already on the telephone. When he had made the arrangements, he turned back to them. "Listen, there's one other thing. A horde of reporters are cooling their heels outside. I'm going to ask you not to make a statement no matter how much they badger you."

"I understand," Marsh said again. He rose with the sleeping child. "Come on, Patty. And Suzanne. It's time to get some sleep."

Sleep. The word sounded good to Phil. He'd been at the station since morning. There would be no medals for his hours of overtime. Why had he not gone home?

Because, he realized, the case was intriguing—and having come this far, he wasn't about to turn it over. He would check out Shannon's story himself.

The Pulaski County hall of records in Arkansas would be open at 8 a.m., 6 a.m. Pacific time. That didn't leave much time for sleep. But after he called he'd know for certain if that doe-eyed woman was lying—and he found himself betting she was not. Her story was just cockamamie enough for him to believe she was telling the truth.

As he headed for his Jeep, he saw the crush of reporters clustered around the Marshes. As he'd instructed, the deputies hustled them into the car. He hoped Daniel Marsh had kept his word and not made a statement tonight.

It was a seventeen-mile drive inland to Salinas—as close to the sea as he could afford to live. But when he pulled into his driveway, the house looked darker and less inviting than usual.

He'd never expected to end up a bachelor. It still surprised him that he had. He'd expected to marry Theresa Ames, the most popular girl in his high school class. She had worn his class ring, was still wearing it when she left for a job as a news writer on a television station in San Francisco. She'd worked her way up from doing brief spots on the air to an anchor position. She was Terry Ames now, and somewhere along the line she had returned his ring.

He still found himself smiling back at her when she smiled out at the world doing the evening news. Sometimes, exasperated with himself, he'd flip to another channel. But the next night he'd find himself smiling back again at her despite himself.

There had been romance since then. God, he'd tried. But every time he'd convinced himself he was getting interested in someone, he'd find himself back in front of the TV, staring at Theresa and wishing. Stupid, he told himself time and again, but what the hell, he had the job.

As he turned the key in the lock, Moe started screeching, chastising him for being late. "Stuff it, bird." He tossed his jacket on a chair. "I'm hungrier than you are."

But he fed the cockatiel first, then built himself a ham, cheese, and chili pepper sandwich. Heading for the living room, he turned on the three-way lamp, leaving it on dim. He sat in the chair that faced the sea—or his version of it. One wall was painted blue and on it he'd mounted his model ships, each one on its own small shelf. His occasional guests sometimes teased him, saying they could get seasick staring at the wall, but when he was in the right mood, he loved it. He wasn't in the right mood tonight.

He ate his sandwich, wishing he'd bothered to open a beer, but he wasn't going back to the kitchen. He took a last bite of sandwich, then stretched out on the couch. Already half asleep, he reached over and switched off the lamp, knowing he would awaken at six without the help of an alarm clock.

At a few minutes after six he was dialing the phone. Area code 501. He identified himself and explained what he wanted to know. The voice on the other end was feminine and languid, pacing that seemed to belong to another world.

It took forever. He almost felt as if he could have made a round trip to Arkansas himself before he heard the drawling voice again. But what she told him made up for the wait. He hadn't expected to feel so relieved. He found himself thanking her with more enthusiasm than was probably necessary.

❧ 6 ❧

For Shannon Buchanan it was a long, sleepless night. Everything seemed unreal, as if she were caught in the throes of a nightmare. They'd been so happy, the two of them singing, and it had happened so fast. Shannon cried, thinking how frightened Mandy must be without her. She felt crushed—helpless—but something in the rosy beginnings of dawn filled her with new resolve.

It had been hard to tell Investigator Tewkes about Arkansas, but she'd had no choice, not if strangers were claiming Mandy was theirs. Shannon sighed, staring out the small window of the cell. At least Tewkes had listened to her.

If Trevor had listened—really listened—if he'd even tried to realize how she felt about the baby she was carrying, none of this would have happened.

Trevor. She rarely thought about him now, but suddenly she could visualize him. He'd been concerned about her, but adamant, too, insisting she have an abortion. "It's the only way, Summer. You're young and free and your whole life is ahead of you. A baby would only tie you down."

"But I want the baby, Trevor," she'd repeated.

"No, you don't. Not really," he argued. When she broke down he comforted her, but he didn't change his mind. The next day he brought her a present—a used, blue Pinto.

"After you go to the clinic you'll have something of your own to drive around in," he'd said. "That ought to cheer you up."

Seeing the Pinto made her realize, finally, that he would not change his mind. And although she wanted badly to please him, she could not change hers, either.

Early on the morning of her appointment at the clinic, she drove mindlessly along the beach—then impulsively drove back to her rooming house to pack her belongings. It was not until she reached the highway that she thought about where she would go.

She decided on Atlanta because she knew her way around there, and she knew she could earn some money. She was not at all surprised to get her old job back—it was as though it had been waiting for her to claim it. She saved her money as she had done before—only this time it was for Mandy.

She knew the child she carried was a girl. She would not have it any other way. In the balmy evenings of that southern spring, sitting on the porch of yet another rooming house, she tried out a thousand names and finally decided on Mandy—Amanda Desiree. How she loved the sound of it! She could hardly wait for Mandy to be born.

But when her pregnancy became too obvious, Mr. Bianco fired her. She had money saved, but without a job she had felt the stirrings of panic. Shannon sighed, remembering. It had been nothing compared to the panic she felt now.

She'd left Atlanta, heading west, but sleeping in the car became increasingly difficult. She didn't feel very well. When she reached Little Rock, she went to a clinic, knowing that her baby would come soon.

"Mandy was born in late October," she'd told Tewkes the evening before. "It was raining when we left the hospital. I didn't know what to do. I had nowhere to take her."

Tewkes had stared at her. "Didn't you ask anyone for help?"

"You mean charity? I didn't want that. I wanted us to manage on our own."

"What did you do?"

She'd hung her head. "There was a department store nearby." Her cheeks flamed. "I only intended to take Mandy in long enough to feed her. I was looking for the ladies' room, and I had to go through the baby department." She'd looked up at him, wanting so badly to make him understand. "There were cribs and cradles and a tiny tub. And the most delicate mobile with stars and moons, and teddy bears, and sweaters, and satin quilts. Things I could never give Mandy. . . ." She'd caught her breath then, realizing how foolish she sounded.

"Then what happened?" Tewkes prompted.

She hung her head again. "There was one cradle—it was white wicker with a satin bow and a fluffy pink quilt. Mandy didn't have a bed, just a basket I'd fixed for her. It had seemed good enough before she was born, but . . . Mr. Tewkes, I don't know what came over me. To this day I don't know why I did it."

"Did what, Shannon?"

"I hid in the ladies' room. Mandy cried a little, but no one paid much attention to us. When the store was closed, I went back to the children's department and"—her voice quivered—"I put Mandy in the cradle."

She'd looked at the investigator again, trying to read his expression. She couldn't. His face was blank.

She'd swallowed. "Alarms went off. I'd triggered electronic sensors or something. The police came and took us to the station, and then—they took Mandy away from me." Her voice rose. "She was only two days old, and they took her away from me! I told them I wasn't trying to steal anything, but I didn't know if they believed me."

"What happened then?" Tewkes' voice was gentle.

"I was weak and shaky, and at the police station I fainted. They took me to the hospital. One of the nurses told me not to worry, that Mandy was in a foster home and would get good care. The nurse knew the woman who had her. Told me she lived only a block away, in the big house on the corner of Front Street and Oakley."

Her words tumbled out, as if, having told him this much, she couldn't get the words out quickly enough. "The next day I felt stronger. I was afraid they would arrest me, and I wouldn't get my baby back. So I dressed and just—walked out. I walked back to the department store and got my car from the lot and then I drove to Front Street and Oakley and found the house. The door was unlocked. I could hear water running in the kitchen. I went in. Mandy was sleeping in a bedroom. I . . . I picked her up and ran. I put her in the basket on the front seat of the Pinto and drove until I had to stop for gas."

Shannon hadn't been able to stop crying. "Don't you see," she begged Tewkes. "I didn't steal Mandy. She's mine! But when you said—when you told me you thought I'd stolen a baby . . . I thought . . ."

Suddenly, he threw up his hands. "How dumb can anybody be, Buchanan? Don't you know the authorities could have helped you? The courts hadn't taken custody of Mandy. You could have gotten help. You hadn't committed a crime in that store. They wouldn't have booked you for anything."

She stared at him. "I didn't know that. I was scared . . . like I'm scared now."

Tewkes shook his head. "If you're telling the truth, you don't need to be scared. First thing in the morning I'll call the Arkansas Recorder's Office and see if they can confirm your story about Mandy's birth."

"Wait!" she called as he turned to go. "Remember, on her birth certificate my name is Summer Knight. But when I left Arkansas, I couldn't sign my pictures that way anymore, so I changed my name again—to Shannon Buchanan."

The suggestion of a smile had played at his lips. "Beats Valeria Valentine," he said.

He'd left them, and it had been a long wait until morning.

Shannon continued to pace her cell. Tewkes could have called Arkansas by now. She was sure he'd be coming soon to tell her he knew Mandy was hers. The nightmare would be over, and they would be free to go.

Roger Connelly was surprised when Terry Ames phoned asking for an early morning interview.

"Mr. Connelly, this is Terry Ames at KBX. I know it's awfully early to be calling, but we'd like to do an interview with you for the morning news."

Roger blinked awake. "Terry?" he questioned. "Why, what's up?"

"It's the Marsh case—the child who was recovered and returned to her parents yesterday. We'd like to get your views and possibly some insights into the police work that was done."

Roger hesitated. "Terry, under the circumstances the people you should be talking to are the police."

"Maybe," she responded, "but our information is that you encouraged the police to release the child to the Marshes—that you've taken a personal interest in the case."

"Terry, I'm the interim district attorney. I'm interested in *all* criminal cases in the county." He paused. "If you want to do an interview—okay. But at least give me time to shave."

Terry laughed. "We won't be there for an hour. And Mr. Connelly—Roger—I bet you'd look great even without a shave."

Roger hung up the phone. He'd known Terry for a long time. She was definitely in his camp, and though he wasn't eager, he'd do the interview for her.

He dressed, choosing a blue sport shirt left open at the neck. Later, Lorelei joined him, looking magnificent in a cream-colored peignoir, her black hair cascading down her back.

She patted him on the arm. "I called Neely. He's coming right over. He'll be here before Terry Ames arrives."

Roger turned to look at her. "Why did you do that?"

She shrugged. "I thought you'd want him here. He—well, he

knows how to handle things for you. Get you prepared before you face the cameras."

He started to tell her that he was perfectly capable of handling things on his own. But what did it matter? Maybe it wouldn't be a bad idea to have Neely around.

As if on cue, Neely arrived, coming around the house to be let in through the patio door. Tall, blond, and impeccably groomed even this early in the morning, he flashed his friend the good-humored, languid smile that had been his trademark since college.

Roger nodded. "Thanks for coming to help out."

"Anytime," Neely responded. "Now, tell me all you know about the case. Let's get a few responses ready."

Roger looked at him. "Almost all I know about the case is what you told me when you called yesterday. That a transient had been picked up with a child who'd been kidnapped—where? In Salinas, wasn't it?"

"Yes, last July in a department store."

"You certainly have all the details down pat, don't you, Neely?"

Neely glanced away. "I always do my homework, Rog. You know that."

They rehearsed for a few minutes, Neely firing questions and Roger struggling with answers. He liked people and enjoyed talking, but the artificiality of the camera bothered him. And there was always the danger of saying too much or the wrong thing.

But Neely was assuring him he would do fine. Lorelei had left them alone, but now she reappeared. She'd changed clothes, replacing the peignoir with a green silky-looking pants suit.

Neely whistled his appreciation. "You'll make a fabulous governor's wife."

"You say that as if it were an accomplished fact." Roger walked to the floor-to-ceiling glass that made up one wall of his living room, and he gazed out over the ocean. "You've almost got me convinced."

Neely laughed. "You were already convinced when we were in college, but I'll help all I can if you'll let me."

"Daddy."

Roger turned and saw Kelly, dressed in bunny-suit pajamas, standing with her arms extended, wanting to be picked up. He hoisted her into the air. "How's Daddy's little girl?"

"Hungry, Daddy. I'm hungry."

"Well, it's early for you to be up, but let's see if Mrs. Flanders is here—"

Neely interrupted. "Let me take her to the kitchen and get her something to eat. It's time she found out her godfather is the world's best pancake chef."

Roger hadn't heard Lorelei let Terry Ames in, but as he turned to hand the child to Neely, he saw her standing in the doorway.

"Good morning," she said. "Sorry to barge in on you at this hour, but I'm glad you understand. We'd like to have the segment for the early news broadcast—all the way down the coast to San Diego. The van will be here in a couple of minutes."

She stared at the child. "Roger, she's adorable—a real asset to your campaign."

Roger kissed Kelly on the cheek, then gave her to Neely, who took her into the kitchen. He turned to Terry. "She's our pride and joy, Terry, but she's a Connelly, not a Kennedy. She's not going to grow up in the limelight with reporters tracking her . . . even pretty reporters. . . ."

He stopped, listening as the van pulled into the driveway.

"Let's film at the door, shall we?" Terry said, springing into action. "Mrs. Connelly, would you like to stand alongside your husband? There, on the left. Okay now, boys," she called to the crew, "are we ready?"

Roger was nervous, more nervous than he was willing to admit, but he smiled and looked toward the camera. Terry was talking, then it was his turn.

"It is a pleasure for me to have this opportunity to congratulate the police force publicly. They have done a painstaking, thoroughly professional piece of work, and as a result, there's a reunited family in the state today."

He took a firm hold on Lorelei's arm. "My wife and I are the proud parents of a wonderful little girl, and this morning we share in the Marshes' joy. I'm sure parents everywhere join us in saluting the fine detective work that led to their daughter's safe return."

"Mr. Connelly, can you tell us anything about how the police finally broke the case?"

Roger shook his head. "I really don't have the details. From the early reports, however, it's obvious that the police throughout the state have been cooperating fully with every aspect of the investigation. Frequently the public sees only the final outcome—the tip of the iceberg—of what was in reality months of diligent, painstaking work."

"Yes, Mr. Connelly, but can you give our viewers any specifics? The police haven't made a statement yet, and the question on everyone's mind is what exactly led to the arrest of the suspect."

"I understand there was a tip. A responsible, caring citizen tipped the police—and aided in the investigation. It's something that should be an inspiration to us all."

When the interview was over, Roger felt the strain. He was breathing hard when he finally closed the door.

Neely was in the hallway, nodding his approval. "Well done, you two. You really are a striking couple, and I bet you picked up a few police bloc votes. Kelly's in the kitchen. Come and have some pancakes, and I'll tell you about some new ideas I have for your campaign."

Roger watched as Neely led Lorelei toward the kitchen. He took a deep breath, then followed them.

✕ 7 ✕

THE MORNING WAS HAZY AND overcast in Salinas, but by noon it would probably be hot. It never failed to amaze Phil that, seventeen miles inland, the climate was so vastly different from what it was on the coast.

He stood with his hands on his hips, gazing skyward. He walked toward the Jeep, opened the door, then paused. Maybe he should check the oil. He released the hood and went through the motions. The oil was fine. Of course it was fine. He slammed the hood shut.

It was time to get on with it. He'd felt something akin to satisfaction when he learned from the Pulaski County records clerk that Buchanan had, in fact, given birth to Mandy in Arkansas, as she'd said. From the first time he'd talked to her, despite her evasions and AKA's, he had felt she told the truth about that.

But it followed that, if she was the child's mother, then Patty Marsh was not. Still, he'd let the Marshes take custody of her overnight—hoping, he realized, that after spending time with the child, they might realize she wasn't theirs. It had seemed like a good idea at midnight, but now, in the light of day, he was afraid he'd made a mistake.

Suppose the Marshes couldn't admit the child wasn't their missing daughter. Worse yet, what if they really believed she was?

He backed the Jeep out of the driveway. There was only one way to find out.

He hadn't driven a block when it dawned on him he was hearing Connelly's voice. He had turned on the radio without paying it much mind, but now he was alert to the familiar voice, his attention riveted to the words: ". . . parents everywhere join us in saluting the fine detective work that led to their daughter's safe return. . . ."

What in the name of everything holy! Phil pressed the accelerator to the floor. He thought he'd made it clear to the district attorney that it was too soon for a statement.

He careened into the parking lot of the sheriff's station, parked the Jeep, and slammed the door shut behind him, striding past the clutch of reporters without a glance in their direction. He headed straight for his superior's office.

Investigative Sergeant Lawler was on the phone. Phil leaned forward, bracing his hands on the desk, demanding Lawler's attention.

Lawler glanced up, his ruddy face questioning. "Look," he said, "I'll call you back." Then he turned his attention to Phil. "What ate you for breakfast?"

"Who in this station has been giving out statements about the kid we took in last night?"

"The Marsh kid?"

"Dammit, she's *not* the Marsh kid!" Phil shouted, banging a fist on the desk. "Nobody ever said she was! On what basis did Connelly go public?"

"Hold it, Phil. *You* released her to the Marshes' custody."

"Overnight," Phil muttered. "I guess I was hoping they'd either be able to make a positive ID or realize the whole thing was a mistake."

He paced the small office. "As it turns out, I *have* positive ID. The child we picked up is Amanda Knight and Buchanan is her mother. The birth certificate is on file in Pulaski County, Arkansas. There's a certified copy on its way here."

Lawler, all two hundred and ten pounds of him, stood up and came around the desk. "Wait a minute, Phil. You're getting ahead of me. What's this about a birth certificate?"

Phil grimaced, trying to stay calm. "Before I left her last night, the Buchanan woman finally opened up—told me when and where the kid was born. Early this morning I checked it out. It appears we've made a mistake. Despite the resemblance, the child we picked up last night is Amanda Knight—not the missing Marsh child."

Lawler whistled softly and walked back around the desk to sit heavily in his chair. "What about the Marshes? Do they know? Have you talked to them since last night?"

Phil shook his head. "No, not yet . . . I'm not looking forward to talking to them."

Lawler leaned forward. "You blew it, Phil. You never should have released her. Now, no matter what we do, we're going to come out the heavies. The newspapers are full of the story, the public is waving flags for the Marshes, and Connelly's giving interviews congratulating us—"

Phil looked at his superior. "I know, I know. And the press is having a field day with it. But it looks like we'll have to bite the bullet and admit a mistake's been made. . . ."

Lawler nodded. "The DA's gonna charge like a wounded bull. We screwed up and, as a result, he went public and made a fool of himself. Listen, before we do anything else, I want to see that birth certificate. And try and get the Marshes to acknowledge that the kid isn't theirs."

Lawler picked up the phone. "I'll try to reach Connelly and let him know what's happened. Just as well to do it on the phone. Give him a chance to cool down before I see him in person."

Walking out of the room, Phil cursed his own stupidity. After so many years on the job, he should have learned to be more cautious. He'd been quick to chastise Vaughn for calling the Marshes, but he himself had made the bigger mistake. He hoped the

Marshes had already realized that this child was not their daughter.

Phil knew he should head straight for the Marshes, but God, it was going to be hard. Maybe he should give them more time with the child. Knowing full well he was rationalizing, he decided to go and see Buchanan first. After all, she didn't even know he'd corroborated her story. At least he could put her out of her misery by telling her her story checked out.

He drove the seventeen miles to the county jail and pulled into a police space. He expected to find Buchanan alert and pacing, but she was asleep on her bunk, her honey-colored hair flared over her pillow. A second look showed him the dark circles under her eyes. She hadn't been asleep long.

She looked childlike herself, her skin pale—translucent almost, like the mother-of-pearl mast he'd planned to mount on the *Bolívar* model at home. He paused, wondering whether to wake her, but suddenly she sat bolt upright, staring at him with those frightened-doe eyes.

He smiled at her. "It's okay, Buchanan. I called Arkansas this morning. A copy of Mandy's birth certificate is on its way."

She stood and walked unsteadily toward him, her hands grasping the cell bars. "I knew after I talked to you last night that everything would be okay."

He could tell she was struggling to hold back tears but she stood straight, all five feet two or three inches of her, and made a stab at recovering her dignity. "Investigator Tewkes," she said solemnly. "I really want to thank you. I know I've done some dumb things in my life, but nobody else ever really listened to me before— except maybe Mandy."

"No wonder." He grinned at her despite himself. "You have a penchant for bending the truth."

"No, I don't. It was just . . . I was so afraid because of what happened in Arkansas."

"What happened in Arkansas wasn't a crime. I told you that last night."

"Do you have to see the birth certificate before you can let me go?" Her hands tightened around the bars. "Mandy must be scared to death, wondering what happened to me."

"Mandy's fine. Mrs. Forbes, our social worker, said she's never seen another kid that young who can talk up a storm the way Mandy can." Phil chuckled. "Seems she asked for chocolate mouse pie for supper."

"She means chocolate mousse pie. It's her favorite thing. I promised it to her last night," Shannon said. "When can I see her, Mr. Tewkes?"

"Soon, I hope." He hesitated. "There is a complication . . ."

"Those other people—the people you told me about, who think my Mandy might be theirs . . ." The tears she'd struggled against welled in her eyes. "I feel sorry for them, I really do, Mr. Tewkes. But you know Mandy is mine. . . ."

"I'm hoping they know that by now, too, Shannon. I'm going to see them."

"Thank you," she called as he strode down the corridor. "Thank you from the bottom of my heart."

There was no more putting it off, Phil knew as he shoved his way past the reporters. He had put himself in this spot. It was time to follow through.

The motel where they'd sequestered the Marshes was nestled in a grove of Monterey pines. Secluded though it was, Phil was sure the press would track them down. He hoped the motel manager had followed instructions and allowed no one to get near them.

He tapped at the door of room sixteen. "Investigator Tewkes."

Daniel Marsh swung the door wide. "Come in," he said, extending his hand. "The three of us were about ready to head for home. We were beginning to wonder if you'd forgotten us."

The three of us. Phil's shoulders sagged. Nothing was ever easy.

Patty Marsh was seated on the sofa, but the child she held squirmed out of her arms the moment Phil entered the room.

"You took my Shannon." She stamped her foot. "Where is she? I want her!"

Phil studied her face. She looked like Shannon. At least the resemblance was there. Maybe he should have realized that last night despite the photo Vaughn had showed him.

"Shannon's fine, honey," he told her. He braced himself. "Mr. and Mrs. Marsh . . . I know this is hard, but it seems there's been a mistake. We have reason to believe the woman who was picked up with this child is, in fact, her mother. We're waiting for a birth certificate to arrive from Arkansas confirming that the child is Amanda Knight."

Patty Marsh covered her face with her hands, but her husband stepped between Phil and the child. "What are you talking about?" he said gruffly. "She's our Suzanne. No one's taking her away again. I've made a reservation on the two o'clock flight. Suzy's going home with us."

Patty Marsh lowered her hands and looked toward her husband. What was it Phil saw in her expression? He looked at her closely, wondering.

Mandy darted around Daniel Marsh and tugged Phil's pants leg. "I don't like it here. I want my Shannon." Her chin quivered and tears pooled in her eyes. "Where is she? I want to go with Shannon."

Patty Marsh reached for her, but the child struggled out of her grasp. "No, no, I don't want you! I want my Shannon!"

Patty Marsh started to cry. "She doesn't know me. She doesn't remember me at all."

Marsh put his arms around his wife. "It's been a long time, and remember how little she was. We'll all get to know each other again, you'll see."

Phil was stymied. Daniel Marsh seemed more convinced than ever that this was their child. He wasn't fazed by—or even interested in—the Amanda Knight birth certificate. "I know how difficult this is for both of you," Phil began, "and I apologize on behalf of the department for getting you up here before we had a positive identification. But the fact is—"

"We are your positive identification!" Daniel Marsh broke in. "I'm telling you . . . we're telling you . . . this is our daughter."

Phil kept his voice even. "I'm sorry, sir. Our evidence indicates otherwise. We could request blood tests—it may come to that—but when the birth certificate arrives from Arkansas, I don't think blood tests will be necessary."

Steeling himself, Phil reached for the child's hand. "I'm going to take her with me. We'll keep her in protective custody until that birth certificate arrives."

"Please, please," Patty Marsh broke in. "Please don't take her now. Leave her until—until it arrives. Maybe there's a mistake."

"That's it, of course!" her husband agreed. "There's sure to be a mistake. I demand we be allowed to keep custody of Suzy. We won't go home without our daughter."

Relenting despite his better judgment, Phil released the little girl's hand. There was no point in dragging her out of there and turning her over to social workers.

He turned to leave, and with his back toward the Marshes, he said, "Listen, a messenger is expected with that birth certificate sometime this afternoon. When it gets here, I'll come back for the child. I'm sorry, there's nothing else I can do."

Daniel Marsh followed him to the Jeep. "Tewkes, she's Suzy. I'm sure of it! I don't give a damn about blood tests or birth certificates. I'll do whatever I have to do to protect my wife and daughter."

❧ 8 ❧

PHIL TOOK HIS TIME getting back to the station. He needed to do some hard thinking. The Marshes would not give up that child on the strength of a piece of paper. Birth certificate or no, they would have to order blood tests—and other tests if it came to that—to prove the child was actually Amanda Knight.

He didn't want anyone—not Connelly, Lawler, or the Marshes—to claim he had done less than was humanly possible to determine the child's identity. When Shannon took custody of her daughter, he wanted no one to doubt she was the mother.

Phil found a message on his desk—Lawler wanted to see him pronto. But before he could respond, the telephone rang.

"Investigation, Tewkes," he said, answering.

The voice on the other end was chipper. "Tewkes, is it? They tell me you're the one who's investigating the Marsh case."

Phil paused. "That's right."

"Jack Avery, city desk, *L.A. Times.*"

"What can I do for you, Avery?"

"Nothing, actually. But I think I can do something for you. This Buchanan woman. Shannon Buchanan? Claims to be the mother of the child who was with her?"

Phil frowned, flipping open a notebook. "Okay, what is it, Avery?"

"Let me read you an excerpt from an *L.A. Times* piece dated June 25, 1987: 'County paramedics responded to a call yesterday . . .' "

Listening, Phil jotted down the date and began to scrawl across the notepad. He stopped halfway through the impersonal reading, his pen poised in midair.

After he hung up he sat—just sat—staring at the phone. Suddenly, he felt old, tired, and infinitely disgusted.

He rose slowly and walked to the window, needing to see the ocean. The Monterey substation sat on a bluff overlooking the sea—a fact, he had often reflected, the city fathers probably regretted, given the present value of the real estate. For Phil the location, at times like these, almost made his job bearable.

Everything out there now was gray—the sky, the fog, the water. He stood with his hands in his pockets, watching the waves pound the shore. He'd been so sure Buchanan was telling the truth—and she had been, up to a point. The birth certificate would arrive soon. A lot of good it would do. . . .

As he stared at the rolling ocean, his head began to clear. He shook off the grayness that had begun to engulf him. Who was he, anyway? Some celluloid Vaughn, going off half-cocked before he'd checked out the facts?

Briskly, Phil picked up the phone. His voice was harsh and impersonal. He asked for Los Angeles Information. "I want the number of the County Hall of Records."

He placed the call, identified himself, and explained what he needed to know. Then he waited, as he had that morning, his fingers drumming a tattoo.

But this time, when his inquiry was answered, he felt rocked by emotions he couldn't name—fury, disappointment, embarrassment. He'd believed her—had wanted to believe her. Maybe he was as crazy as she was.

Slowly, he pulled himself to his feet and moved down the hall to Lawler's office. If he had made a fool of himself, he was man enough to own up to it.

His superior motioned Phil to a seat. "We've got a mess," he said, agitated. "The minute you left Marsh's motel, he called the reporters. He claims the kid is theirs²—that we're irresponsible and they're taking her home with or without police approval. They can't do that, of course, but they can scream pretty loud. And they do have physical custody."

Phil smiled dryly. "Is that a reproach?"

"Get off it, Phil," Lawler went on. "When I talked to Connelly, he was pushing to prosecute—and release the kid to the Marshes. But then this came." He held up an envelope.

The birth certificate. Phil slumped in his chair.

"From the beginning you had your doubts about the kid's being Suzanne Marsh. But when we jerk her back and hand her over to a transient, the press, Connelly—everybody will murder us."

Phil started to speak, but Lawler cut him off. "Hear me out, will ya, Phil?"

Phil stared at him dourly as Lawler became expansive. "We'll contact the experts at U.C. Davis. Have them start the HLA blood typing right away on the kid, the Marshes, Buchanan. Let's see what they can find out. Meanwhile, I want you to arrange a lineup. See if Patricia Marsh can pick out Buchanan as the woman she handed her kid to in Salinas. And while you're at it—"

Phil cut him off. He had heard enough. He wanted to be done with it. "Forget the tests. We don't need them. As far as I'm concerned, we've got everything we need. We can send the kid home with the Marshes."

Lawler threw up his hands. "What the hell are you talking about? Why the sudden about-face? Couple hours ago you were waiting for a birth certificate. Now we have it. So now what?"

Phil leaned across the desk and snatched the envelope from Lawler. "We've got a birth certificate, yeah. But it isn't going to matter."

He rose to his feet and jammed his fists in his pockets. "A child was born to the suspect in custody—in Arkansas, just as she said. But the child died, Lawler. Amanda Knight died—of meningitis —two weeks before the Marsh kid was snatched."

Lawler stared. "What are you saying?"

"Her death certificate is on file in Los Angeles."

✻ 9 ✻

SHANNON AWAKENED FROM HER SECOND night in jail convinced it would be her last. By now the birth certificate would have arrived at the Monterey County court house. It would prove she'd had a baby in October 1985, just as she'd said. They would have to let her go. They would have to give Mandy back to her.

She tried not to think about the couple from San Diego who thought Mandy was theirs. They wanted Mandy—who wouldn't want Mandy? But no one could ever prove she wasn't Mandy's real mother.

She didn't have her sketch pad and chalks, but she'd been given paper and pencil. The pencil was hard lead, but she sketched to pass the time. At first she seemed to be blocking out a figure at random, but then she realized it was going to be Investigator Tewkes.

She closed her eyes, visualizing him. He had thick, almost wiry-looking, faded red hair. That would have to be the identifying feature because his face was plain—straight nose, small ears, and wide-set, honest eyes. She finished the drawing by adding a few exaggerated freckles. She paused a moment, then signed the drawing—*Ruth Ann Stone.*

She would give it to him when he came to see her. Maybe, in a small way, it would let him know how grateful to him she was for checking out her story. It was his job, of course, but she still appreciated it.

She put the finished drawing aside and paced her cell. She was lonesome for Mandy, frustrated from being cooped up for so long, but soon Tewkes would come and tell her she was free to go and could take Mandy with her.

"Buchanan! Hey, Buchanan!" Shannon turned to see a pretty girl housed in a nearby cell returning from a conference in the visiting room. The matron had barely left the area when she hissed at Shannon again from across the corridor. "You know that kid you said was yours? Well, honey, you got problems! My boyfriend told me he saw pictures on TV last night—they showed that couple from San Diego gettin' on a plane with the kid."

Shannon flung herself toward the bars. "Mandy? They've taken Mandy?"

"Showed the district attorney congratulating the sheriff—reporters, the whole number . . ."

Shannon didn't hear any more. The world trembled around her. She lay down on the bed, wishing the spinning would stop, wishing she could clear her head and think. *Tewkes knew Mandy was hers. Why would he have let the Marshes take her baby?*

Patty Marsh had been all but oblivious to the reporters who'd swarmed around them at the San Diego airport when they'd landed on Friday evening. Clutching Suzanne, she and Daniel had plowed their way through the crush and taken a taxi home. More reporters had been waiting on their doorstep, but Daniel had held them at bay, answering their questions while she escaped into the house carrying Suzanne.

Inside, she put the little girl on her feet. For a moment, standing in her own hallway, Patty felt close to collapse. Then Daniel's mother and Danny Joe rushed to greet them, and she steeled herself again.

"Suzy, this is Grandma Stella," she said. "You remember her, don't you? And Danny Joe?"

Danny Joe rushed to his mother, but Stella, crying, reached for the little girl. "Suzy—thank God. Let Grandma see you."

She pulled away. "I want my Shannon," she said, retreating behind Patty's skirt.

"It's all right, sweetheart." Stella knelt by the child. "You don't remember me, but I remember you. My, how tall you are. And you're so thin now. We'll have to fatten you up, won't we, Mommy? And those overalls! You'll look more like our Suzy when we get you back in pretty dresses."

Turning away from them, Patty picked up Danny Joe. "How's Mommy's big boy? I missed you."

"Is she my sister?" Danny Joe returned his mother's hug, but his attention was focused on the little girl.

Daniel came in then, pushing the door closed behind him. "Hi, sport. How's my guy?" He lifted Danny Joe into the air and, still holding him, leaned over to kiss his mother.

"Come on, Suzy," said Patty, taking her small hand. "Maybe Daddy will help Grandma and Danny Joe make us something to eat while you and I get cleaned up. I'll give you a nice bubble bath, and then we'll look for something else for you to wear."

In the bathroom, she closed the door firmly and undressed the child while the tub filled with water. She stared at the little body, noticing again that she was a slender child now, no longer a chubby baby. She was such a little thing, and she'd been such a big baby. But of course the baby fat would have disappeared. No reason to wonder at that.

Deliberately shifting her thoughts, Patty picked up the child and put her into the mound of bubbles.

For the first time the child seemed happy, splashing in the water, playing with the bubbles, and keeping up a steady stream of chatter. Patty watched her closely and answered her questions until she asked, "When my Shannon comes, can she have a bath with bubbles?"

Patty tensed. "Shannon isn't coming. You're my little girl."

A tiny mound of bubbles coated the child's chin. "Oh, yes, Shannon will come."

Patty carried the towel-draped child into the pink and white bedroom and paused, staring at the crib. "Suzy, you're too big for that now. Tomorrow we will buy you a bed. And new clothes too. Pretty dresses and new shoes."

Suddenly, she stopped and caught her breath. *Shoes.* That's what she had just bought for her Suzy the day—the day she'd been stolen. Impulsively, she hugged Suzanne until the child pushed at her, gasping for breath.

Sitting the child on a dressing table, Patty went to get the shoes. They were patent-leather T-straps with shiny buckles. Patty held them in her hands. Her heart pounding, she looked at the shoes, then at the child's tiny feet.

Feeling as if she were trapped in a slow-motion dream, Patty slipped one shoe onto the foot the child extended. It should be too small. It had to be too small—but it wasn't. It went right on. Eleven months later, and the shoe still fit.

Patty felt an unbearable pressure. *But Daniel was so certain.* She shook her head, fighting off dizziness. "No," she moaned. "You have to be Suzy. You have to be."

The little girl started to cry. "My name is Mandy," she wailed. "Mandadesiree Knight. I know it is. Shannon told me."

"Patty." Daniel was standing in the doorway, holding a newspaper, his face ashen. "It's all here. It . . . it explains everything."

Slowly, as if still trapped in the dream, Patty reached for the paper:

Child of Kidnapping Suspect Dead

Shannon Buchanan, currently held in a Salinas jail, is now the prime suspect in the kidnapping of Suzanne Marsh from a Salinas shopping mall last July. Buchanan, investigation re-

vealed, was the mother of a child who died in Los Angeles
several weeks before the kidnapping took place.

Records indicate that Buchanan's daughter, Amanda Desiree
Knight, who would have been three months older than the
Marsh child, died of meningitis.

Charges against Buchanan are expected to be filed . . .

Patty caught her breath, then exhaled slowly. "The woman
must have been crazed with grief," she murmured.

Suddenly, the overwhelming pressure dissolved. She smiled
and, unmindful of the tears running down her own cheeks, she
tried to comfort the child.

"We're strange with each other now. That's all it is. But we'll
get to know each other again. You're my dear Suzy, and I'm your
mommy. Don't cry. You're home, and everything is all right.
Everything is all right at last."

The morning was overcast as Phil turned the Jeep toward the
county jail in Salinas. The previous night he had stared at the
television, watching Theresa do her spiel on the recovery of the
Marsh child. He'd turned off the set in disgust, then made a stab
at working on his model, but his mind had been elsewhere.

The Buchanan woman was an enigma to him. She seemed normal, rational when he talked to her, but maybe she was truly
psychotic. He was not a shrink, but it seemed possible to him that
when her own child died, she had stolen the Marsh child while in
a crazed state of grief. The question was, did she know she had
kidnapped a child or did she believe Suzanne Marsh was actually
the dead Amanda? That's what he hoped to determine when he
talked to her.

Maybe the fact that on Monday she was going to be charged
with felony kidnapping, coupled with the information that Suzanne
Marsh had been released to her parents, would force her to face
reality.

He signed in at the jail, requesting that Buchanan be brought to the visiting room. He cursed under his breath when the matron told him that Buchanan had learned of the child's departure and had had to be physically restrained.

"We've asked for a tranquilizer," the matron said. "She screamed like a wounded banshee."

He waited in the visitor's room, a bleak, square place with sea-green walls that reminded him of anything but the sea.

When Shannon was brought in she was subdued, her eyes dark hollows in an ashen face. She carried a rolled-up sheet of paper, which she tossed carelessly on the table. "I made this for you when I thought you were my friend." She stared at him accusingly. "You let them take my baby away. I thought I could trust you. How could you?"

"Hold on, Buchanan," he told her softly. "The decision to release her was based on the evidence—all the evidence—we had."

"But the birth certificate—you got it, didn't you? It proves Mandy is mine!"

Phil groaned. "Sit down, Shannon. We've got a lot to talk about." He pulled two chairs to the same side of the table and motioned for her to sit.

She moved slowly, watching him warily, circled the chair, then sat. He sat alongside her and cleared his throat. There was nothing to do but say it.

"Look, Shannon, we got the birth certificate from Arkansas, just as you said. Okay, you had a child . . . do you want to talk about what happened to her?"

She looked puzzled. "What do you mean? I told you. I took her into that department store and then . . . well, I told you everything that happened."

"After that, Shannon. Then what happened? In Los Angeles when Mandy got sick?"

Shannon cocked her head. "I don't know what you mean. Mandy's never been sick. Well, she had a cold one time in Texas and I took her to see a doctor. But not in Los Angeles. We were only there a few weeks. Mandy wasn't sick."

"Think, Shannon." Phil prodded her gently. "June 1987. You

and Mandy were in Los Angeles, and Mandy was very sick. Now do you remember? She was taken to a hospital. Can you tell me what happened then?"

Shannon rose, shaking her head. "I . . . I don't know what you're talking about. I was in Los Angeles last June, but Mandy was never in a hospital. Don't you think I would remember?"

"Shannon, sit down," Phil urged. He kept his voice calm, but he felt an anchor weigh on his chest. "My work on this case is finished, and I'm going to talk to you like a friend. God knows you need one."

He took her hand. "Later this week you're going to come up for arraignment in municipal court on charges of felony kidnapping. A public defender will be assigned to your case and—"

Shannon jumped up again, this time knocking over her chair. "Kidnapping! Mandy is mine! You just said you had her birth certificate!"

"Please, Shannon, try to listen." He righted her chair and gently nudged her into it. "Trust me. Will you try to trust me?"

She was breathing hard, her eyes wild, but she nodded, making an obvious effort to calm down. He waited until she seemed to have a grip on herself. Maybe he was making a mistake, but it seemed like the moment to try and get through to her. Perhaps he could get her to come to terms with what had happened.

He took a deep breath. "On June 26, 1987, a death certificate was filed in Los Angeles. Mandy is dead, Shannon. She died of meningitis. I know it's hard, but you've got to be honest—with yourself and with the public defender. Maybe when you took Suzanne Marsh, you didn't know what you were doing."

She was staring at him, her face twisted. She opened her mouth, but no sound came for a moment. Then she started to cry, a keening wail that ended in a single syllable: "No!"

He put his hand on her shoulder to steady her, but she jerked away. "Mandy isn't dead! You're trying to steal her for that couple from San Diego. They must be paying lots of money . . . but Mandy is alive and she's mine!"

Phil was sorry now he'd told her about the death certificate.

She wasn't ready to handle it. Standing up, he leaned over her chair and tried to soothe her.

Suddenly, she jumped up and began to beat his chest with her fists. Sobbing, she repeated over and over, "Mandy's mine, Mandy's mine, Mandy's mine!"

Phil stood like a brick wall, not feeling the blows. He could not remember having ever felt so useless. For a moment he shared her pain.

The matron rushed in, followed by a guard, who grabbed Shannon by the arms and dragged her out of the room.

"You okay?" the matron asked Phil.

"Yeah," he muttered. "I'm fine."

"This one's a loony. A real loony." The matron shook her head as she left.

Phil picked up the roll of paper Shannon had dropped on the table. Unrolling it, he saw a pencil drawing. It was him. An unmistakable likeness.

❧ 10 ❧

On Saturday afternoon Neely Smith felt like lighting fireworks and cheering as they blazed across the sky. He'd been trapped in a desperate situation and worried sick, but sharp brains and dumb luck had combined to see him through. He was at home and feeling relaxed, or almost so, for the first time in weeks.

He dressed carefully but casually in a Pierre Cardin jogging suit, then tidied up the small kitchen. The condo was sparsely furnished—the sky-high rent left him with little money for trimmings—but the Monterey Bay address was worth it. Closing the day bed, he tossed the cushions in place, then left the condo and walked the two blocks to the marina.

He bought the *San Francisco Chronicle* and the *Salinas Californian* and was pleased to see the story was on the first page of both. Deliberately, he tucked the papers under his arm and walked down the pier to board the *Lorelei II* and read the details in private.

He spent more time on the boat than Roger did, and he enjoyed imagining it was his. Easing into a deck chair out of the direct sunlight, he unfolded the *Chronicle* and studied a picture of Daniel and Patty Marsh embracing a golden-haired little girl. Then he scanned the accompanying stories:

San Diego Parents Reunited
with Kidnapped Daughter

In a tearful scene at Salinas county jail on Thursday night, Daniel and Patricia Marsh of San Diego were reunited with their daughter, Suzanne, who was abducted from a Salinas department store nearly a year ago . . .

Bay Area Businessmen Join
Find the Children Campaign

In the wake of the recovery of Suzanne Marsh, who was identified and returned to her parents as a result of milk-carton publicity, several Bay area manufacturers have pledged to print pictures of missing children on their packaging. Ace Grocery Supply, which supplies paper bags to five major supermarket chain stores . . .

Mayor Asks Funds for
Missing Children Posters

Mayor Art Agnos today asked the board of supervisors to approve funds for posters of missing children to be placed on municipal buses and cable cars . . .

He smiled, knowing that future photos of Suzanne Marsh would have "FOUND!" emblazoned across them.

It had been little more than a spur-of-the-moment plan, a long shot, but it had worked. He almost wished there was someone he could share it with, someone who could appreciate his daring.

He'd felt a surge of panic yesterday morning when Lorelei called saying Roger was going to do an interview about the case. He'd rushed over, alert to the danger, but it had gone as smoothly as if he'd planned it.

Roger had complimented him on his knowledge of the details

in the Marsh case. Of course he knew the details, but even now Neely shuddered to think what would happen if Roger ever found out *why* he did.

He stopped reading, aware suddenly of the sound of the gulls, and he watched them as they swooped for their dinner.

He and Roger Connelly went back a long way together. They were both Californians, but they had met at Princeton as freshmen. Neely had admired Roger—envied him, really—from their first encounter, though he had never expected to belong to Roger's crowd. But Roger had singled him out, had seemed to enjoy his friendship, and he'd smoothed Neely's way into his club and made him one of the crowd.

So Arlington Cornelius Smith, son of a construction worker and a department store clerk who studied the society pages and sprinkled her conversation with the first names and activities of socialites she would never meet, got a taste of the good life.

Occasionally, he wrote Roger's papers for him or helped him cram for exams. There wasn't anything he wouldn't have done for Roger, and Roger responded in kind.

Their friendship had even survived that incident at Princeton, but afterward they had gone to different law schools. Eventually, Roger returned to his family's money and position in California, and Neely tried his luck in New York.

When Neely finally realized his star would never rise in the East, he'd returned to California. He had settled in Los Angeles, but after he'd proved he could make himself useful, Roger had suggested he move to the Bay. Now Neely hung close, and he'd all but assumed the role of campaign manager for Roger's run for the governor's office.

Neely looked down at the newspaper in his lap. Just as he'd established himself in the lifestyle he yearned for, *this* had happened. It had been a blow, but it hadn't finished him. He had managed to get out of it.

Again, Neely wished there was someone he could tell, someone who could appreciate his ingenuity—and the irony of it all.

*   *   *

"I think you'll like this cheery yellow room much better than the pink one, Suzy." Patty Marsh dipped a brush into the roller pan and carefully painted the windowsill. "We'll find some pretty gingham curtains, and we'll never even know it's the same room."

The child was seated at a small red table and did not look up from her drawing. "Yellow is Shannon's bestest color. I like yellow too."

Patty bit her lip. Shannon. Always Shannon. "How would you like to go shopping with me tomorrow? Just the two of us. We'll have lunch. And then we'll pick out the curtains and a bed-spread. . . ." She turned to see Suzy put down her crayon.

"Where is Kit Kat? I'll go find her. Maybe she wants to play." She ran out of the room.

Patty resisted the urge to go after her, but she felt a hollow place near her heart.

She had taped the windowpanes and was ready to paint the frame when the phone rang. Laying the brush across the top of the paint can, she hurried to answer it on the extension in her bedroom.

"Mrs. Marsh? My name is Penny Stewart. I'm the president of the Goddard Preschool parents' group. I hope I'm not disturbing you."

Patty sat on the edge of her bed. "No. It's all right. What can I do for you?"

"First, I'd like to say—for all of us—how happy we are for you and Mr. Marsh and for Suzy. And if it's not too soon—I mean, if you feel you're up to it—we'd like to ask you for a favor."

The woman sounded warm and genuinely friendly, and Patty answered, "I'll help you if I can. My husband wants our son to go to Goddard."

"It's a wonderful school. And the parent group is very active —not only in the school but in the community. As a matter of fact, that's why I called. We're planning a fund-raiser for Find the Chil-dren. We wondered if you would be our guest speaker."

Patty hesitated. "Me? You want me to speak?"

"We know you must be eager to help other families with missing children, and, frankly, we need you to draw a crowd. The meeting is set for next Friday evening—seven-thirty, at the community center. Please, if it's not asking too much . . ."

Patty tensed, knowing it would be difficult to speak to a crowd of strangers. *But if it hadn't been for Find the Children . . .* She cleared her throat. "If you think it will help, I'll . . . I'll do it."

She heard Suzy cry out. "Mrs. Stewart—please call me back later." Hanging up, she hurried back to the bedroom.

The child stood in a puddle of paint, obviously terrified, her little hands clasped over her mouth. The paint bucket lay on its side at her feet, oozing its yellow contents in lazy swirls.

Patty righted the paint can, then reached for the trembling child. "It's all right, honey. There's no harm done. Look, the paint is all on the drop cloth." She smoothed Suzy's hair and tried to pull her close.

The little girl pushed away and started to cry. "Shannon. I want my Shannon."

Patty squeezed her eyes shut to keep back tears. "Honey, hold on to me. I'll take care of you. . . ." Dropping to her knees beside the child, she tried again to hug her. This time she felt little arms reach around her neck, and the long remembered contact reassured her.

Of course the child called for Shannon. Shannon was all she remembered. But children were adaptable, marvelously adaptable. Suzy had learned to depend on Shannon, but with love and time, Patty knew she would learn to rely on her again.

She cuddled the child. "Don't cry, Suzy. Mommy is here. Mommy is here."

On Monday, Shannon tried to make herself as presentable as possible for her interview with the public defender. She combed her long, honey-blond hair so that it fell neatly down her back and smoothed the drab blue dress she'd been issued in jail. She had to make the right impression—she had to convince someone she was telling the truth.

She had gone to pieces when Tewkes told her about the death

certificate, but later she'd realized that maybe another little girl named Amanda Knight had died. She just had to prove that it hadn't been her Mandy. Thank God, her Mandy was still alive.

She paced in her cell and twice asked the matron when the public defender was coming, but she was told only that it would be sometime that day.

She was half out of her mind with impatience when she was finally taken to the visiting room. She was surprised but pleased to find that the public defender was female, and she felt something akin to relief as she faced the tall young woman.

"Hello, Miss Buchanan, my name is Rita Taylor. I've been appointed to represent you at your arraignment." The woman gazed at her with clear green eyes framed with owlish glasses. She wore a crisp, beige linen suit and her dark hair was cropped short. "We have a lot to talk about, and I'd like to begin with—"

But Shannon couldn't wait. "The death certificate is a lie, Miss Taylor—or it's for another Amanda Knight. It's not for my Mandy, and you have to help me prove it!"

"Sit down, Miss Buchanan. We'll get to that. First, you should understand what's at stake here."

Shannon sat on the edge of a chair, leaning forward impatiently. The woman reached into a tan leather briefcase and removed a sheaf of papers. "When you appear before a judge in municipal court, you will be charged with kidnapping, which is a felony. You will be asked to enter a plea of guilty or not guilty. What do you want to plead?"

Shannon sat tall in her chair. "Of course, not guilty. I just told you. My Mandy is still alive, and I am not guilty, Miss Taylor."

Rita Taylor took off her glasses and leaned back in her seat. "Suppose you tell me, from the beginning, how you came to have that little girl in your custody."

Slowly, careful not to leave out anything, Shannon repeated the story of Mandy's birth just as she had told it to Phil Tewkes —including taking Mandy from foster care after she left the hospital in Arkansas.

"We left Arkansas and headed west. We were in Texas about

a year and a half, in a small town near Amarillo—Dumas it's called. Then I did go to Los Angeles. I was there on the date Investigator Tewkes said the death certificate was filed—but then I went back to Texas. All you have to do is get in touch with the people I knew in Texas. They can tell you the child I returned with is my Mandy—the same child I left with. That'll be proof, don't you see?" Shannon's voice rose eagerly.

Rita Taylor raised her eyebrows. "You're admitting that you were in California in June of 1987? And were you in Salinas on July 19?"

"No! I was never in Salinas. I was back in Texas on the nineteenth. We left California on the Fourth of July. I remember telling Mandy all the flags were out to say good-bye to us."

The public defender took a sheet of paper from her briefcase. "Shannon, I want you to take a good look at this. It's a photocopy of the death certificate that's on file in Los Angeles."

Shannon snatched it, then stared in disbelief. The name of the deceased was Amanda Knight; birthplace, Little Rock, Arkansas. Mother's name—Shannon Knight, birthplace, Detroit, Michigan.

Fighting a wave of dizziness, Shannon faced Rita Taylor. "My daughter didn't die, Miss Taylor. I think the police are trying to steal her and give her to the Marshes."

Rita Taylor nodded, and when she spoke her voice was soothing. "I see. You think the little girl is your daughter, Mandy, and that the police are trying to steal her from you. Is that right?"

Shannon started to respond, but then stopped. The woman didn't believe her. It was obvious from the tone of her voice.

"Shannon, we'll go into court and enter a plea of not guilty by reason of insanity." Rita Taylor continued, her voice placating, "Can you understand what that means?"

Shannon felt defeated, drained. "Yes," she said, "I can understand that. But, Miss Taylor, I won't plead insanity. I'm not insane; the rest of the world has gone crazy."

His pizza was cold, and a hazy mist was obscuring the sun when Phil Tewkes put the *Bolívar* model aside, washed the glue from his hands, and turned on the six o'clock news. Theresa was wearing a deep red outfit—he'd always loved her in red. Her voice, feminine but clear and precise, was running down the day's events.

He was opening a beer when he caught a glimpse of Shannon's face on the screen.

". . . and today in municipal court, alleged kidnapper Shannon Buchanan entered a plea of not guilty . . ."

Phil dropped heavily into a kitchen chair and strained to get a good look at Shannon. She was pale, but she stood tall and her chin was thrust forward. When she entered her plea, her voice was surprisingly firm. "Not guilty."

Phil recognized the public defender, Rita Taylor, in the last second before the camera cut away. "Taylor," he mused. "She wouldn't be bad." Had a good track record as far as he could remember. But he didn't envy her this assignment.

He reached for the phone. Maybe he could get Taylor at home and talk to her. He stopped. About what? Chewing on a wedge of tasteless pizza, he acknowledged that his involvement in the case was over even if his interest was not. He couldn't help Taylor— he couldn't help Shannon. The doe-eyed girl had gotten to him, but he had to put her out of his mind.

❧ 11 ❧

THE WEATHER COULD NOT HAVE been more perfect for a picnic, Daniel thought, spreading the blanket on a grassy area overlooking the playground. He hadn't signed up to teach summer school because he'd known Patty needed him in her grief. But now, with Suzy returned to them, he looked forward to spending leisurely, happy days with his family.

He could hear Danny Joe's laughter and Suzy's high-pitched squeals of delight as they chased each other around the monkey bars.

Bringing them to the park had been a wonderful idea, but he'd been hesitant about suggesting it, afraid Patty would veto it instantly. To his surprise, she had encouraged him and had even packed them a lunch. She was going to the hairdresser, something she hadn't done in a long time, and then she wanted to do some shopping.

At the last moment she'd tensed. "Daniel, don't let them out of your sight," she pleaded.

He had assured her they would be fine, and he made her promise to spend a carefree day. Now, sitting on the blanket, his long legs bent in front of him, Daniel watched the children playing and was filled with a profound sense of well-being. Everything *would* be fine.

Suzy was finding her niche in the family. She had quickly adopted Kit Kat as her own. She adored Danny Joe and seemed content to follow him, chatting, even when he paid her no mind. She drew back from outright affection, but that seemed natural because she was such an independent little creature.

Suddenly, Daniel stood up, watching as Suzy climbed the steps of the slide. She looked so tiny. He called to her to wait until he could get there to catch her when she came down, but with a dazzling smile in his direction, she let herself whoosh down.

She went right off the slide and landed on her rump, but she was on her feet before he reached her.

"Suzy, are you hurt?"

"Uh-uh, fun. But look. My pretty dress is all dirty." With the manner of a much older person, she brushed sand off her sundress.

"It's okay," he told her. Dirty clothes would not upset Patty, but if Suzy had been injured, Daniel knew the playground would be labeled off-limits.

Daniel hoped that someday Patty's overprotectiveness, like her fears, would vanish, but until then he had to be especially vigilant and keep the children safe from even the normal cuts and bruises. He took Suzy by the hand. "Come on, honey. Let's have lunch."

He called to Danny Joe. "Come on—I'll race you back to the blanket!"

They ate tuna sandwiches and big, ripe strawberries, laughing at each other's attempts to keep the juice from dribbling down their chins. "You look funny, Daddy," Suzy giggled.

"You, too, Suzy," he said.

It startled him to realize that it was nearly noon and Suzy had not mentioned Shannon all day.

The harsh light from the overhead fixtures reflected on Rita Taylor's owlish glasses. Shannon stared at them, mesmerized, thinking how easy it would be to caricature the public defender.

"Shannon, are you listening to me? You have to pay attention."

"Yes, I'm listening. We have ten days until the preliminary hearing." She sighed and tried to concentrate, but all she could think about was Mandy. Her blood ran in Mandy's veins. She knew that. Maybe blood tests could prove it.

"Miss Taylor, I know there are blood tests that can prove if a man *isn't* the father of a child. Are there tests that can prove if a woman is really the mother?"

Rita Taylor shook her head. "I'm not an expert, but from what I understand, HLA blood typing can prove whether a specific couple are—or are not—the parents of a given child."

"A specific couple. Does that mean the tests can't prove I'm her mother unless her father is tested too?"

Rita paused. "I'm not sure, Shannon. I told you I'm not an expert."

Shannon stood up and began to pace back and forth in the visiting room. "Miss Taylor, I want to find out. Can you get me a book that explains all about blood typing?"

"I don't know, Shannon. I could try. But if I got you a medical book that covered the subject, you probably wouldn't be able to understand it. And . . . well, whether you like it or not, we have to consider that blood tests may not help our case one bit."

Rita Taylor hesitated. "However . . . if you consider changing your plea, the district attorney will be sympathetic to your situation. I've talked to him and—"

Shannon cut her off. "Miss Taylor, I won't change my plea. And I *have* to understand about blood tests. I want to know what they can really prove." She didn't want to beg, but the public defender was her only link to the outside world. "Please," she said, her voice strained, "promise me you'll get me the book."

"All right, Shannon—I'll do what I can about a book if you promise to pay attention now so we can get on with this."

Immediately, Shannon took her seat. "What do you want to know?"

"You told me that you left Los Angeles with Mandy on the

Fourth of July and went back to Texas. Shannon, I'm sorry, I really am, but the death certificate on file says Mandy died *before* you went back to Texas."

"The people in Texas *know* I came back with Mandy. Please—talk to them. They'll tell you."

Rita Taylor laid down her pen. "Who can I talk to, Shannon? Where did you live in Texas?"

"With Ida Burke."

"And where does Ida Burke live?"

"She's dead."

Rita put her face in her hands. "You were living with Ida Burke, but Ida Burke is dead?"

"Oh, of course she wasn't dead when I was living with her! But she was eighty-four, Miss Taylor. She died of heart failure one night in her sleep about two months ago. That's when I left Texas for good."

"Okay, Shannon. How long did you live with Ida Burke?"

"All together, over two years. Mandy was a tiny baby when I first moved in with Ida. I cooked and cleaned for her, but I always wanted to move to California, and last summer I decided to try it. I went to Los Angeles—like I told you."

"Then why did you go back to Texas?"

"When I phoned Ida to let her know we were doing okay, she told me she was sick. She missed us and wanted us to come back. She'd been like a grandmother to us, and I had to go back. I took Mandy—my Mandy—and went back."

"Shannon," Rita said softly, "if Ida Burke is dead, there is no way to prove any of this."

Shannon leaned forward, determined. "But Ida had a son. Ray Bob. He still lives in Dumas. He works in his mother's feed store. I guess it's his feed store now. And there are other people in Dumas who know me."

"Do you have addresses or, better yet, telephone numbers where I can reach them? Especially Burke."

Shannon reached for the pad of paper Rita was tapping with her pen. "Here, I'll write Ray Bob's number for you," she said.

Rita Taylor rose to leave. "I'll do what I can."

Shannon stood up too. "Thank you, Miss Taylor. And please, the book—can you get it today? Please, I have no one to ask if you can't do it."

"All right, Shannon. I can stop at the library now—maybe they'll have something. And then I'll put in a call to Texas."

Shannon felt a brief flutter of hope as the public defender left the room. Then she slumped back in her chair. It was no use. Ray Bob wouldn't do anything to help her if his life depended on it. And anyway, she realized, biting her lip, Miss Taylor thought she was crazy. . . .

Later, in the fading rays of the afternoon light, Shannon sat on her cot and leaned back, propping her sketch pad against her knees. She wanted to draw Rita Taylor, but Mandy's sweet face kept swimming before her eyes, and she thought she could hear her crying.

Why did she think that? Mandy rarely cried. Even as a baby, she rarely cried. Shannon smiled. Ida Burke used to say Mandy must have been born under a rainbow, she could put a silver lining in any cloud.

Ida had loved Mandy from the first time she saw her, ten days old and wrapped in a pink blanket.

Amarillo had been just another stop on Shannon's route from Arkansas to California. She had not planned to stay, but her money was low, the roads were slick with autumn rains, and the Pinto needed new tires.

She pulled into a Taco Bell drive-in, nursed Mandy, and counted out change to buy herself a burrito and a pint of milk. Still holding Mandy, she took one bite of burrito. Then, suddenly, she felt so tired she could hardly swallow. Maybe the best thing she could do was stay in Amarillo long enough to rest and earn the money for the tires.

But she needed a place to stay. Sleeping in the car had become an ordeal, and she yearned for a bed—a real bed where she could stretch out and get a decent night's sleep. Putting Mandy down in the little box in the back seat, Shannon sacrificed a quarter to buy a newspaper. She perused the want ads, not even knowing what she hoped to find.

An ad for "temp hskpr—companion, one child OK" caught her attention. It was in Dumas, some forty miles north of Amarillo according to her map, but Shannon decided to brave the rain and try for the job. She called the number and was told to come over for a "look-see." She drove north on Highway 87, and it was night when she found the house.

Smoothing her hair with her hand, she picked up Mandy and went up the stairs to the rambling white house. She tried to perk up, to hide her utter exhaustion, but the first words she ever heard Miss Ida say were "Lord, child—you need help more than I do!"

She woke up the next morning in a comfortable bed, hardly able to remember the previous evening. She was embarrassed, but Miss Ida made her feel at home from that first day.

Miss Ida was tall and bosomy. She wore flowered housedresses and an air of no-nonsense. She took a hand in Mandy's care from the first. "Always wanted a girl baby," she said, "but the Lord saw fit to give me Ray Bob."

The frame house was homey, filled with frilly lampshades and antimacassars like the ones Shannon recalled from her childhood. Shannon helped with the cooking and cleaning, but she realized that Miss Ida had wanted companionship more than assistance. She was past eighty, but still feisty, like the grandmother Shannon remembered.

Their attachment to each other was rapid and genuine, but in her heart Shannon knew that eventually she'd be moving on. She knew Miss Ida sensed it because she kept after Shannon to get a Texas driver's license. Shannon wouldn't do it. It would have been like lying—saying she was going to stay permanently when she knew she wasn't.

It was a peaceful arrangement, though, and Shannon was content to stay through Mandy's babyhood. The only real sore spot was Ray Bob. He lived across town in an apartment over the feed store, but he came to Miss Ida's for Sunday dinner and to borrow money from her.

Shannon could stand it when Miss Ida was around, but she steeled herself those late afternoons when the old woman headed up the stairs for her catnap.

"Hey, goldie-girl," he'd call from the sitting room, "be nice and bring me a beer."

Shannon, up to her elbows in dishwater, would grit her teeth and comply. But no matter how quick she was, Ray Bob's hammy hands would grab at her and force her down on the sofa. She always fought him off by threatening to scream for Miss Ida, but eventually she couldn't put up with it. By the time Mandy was a year and a half, Shannon knew it was time to leave.

She went to California—she was in Los Angeles on the day the death certificate said Mandy had died. Suddenly, Shannon jumped up from her cot. *She had told only one person that she'd been in Los Angeles that day. She visualized him, smiling at her the other day, asking her questions.*

James Johnson.

"Buchanan," a matron called to her. "Your lawyer was just here. Left you a book. God, it weighs more than you do."

❧ *12* ❧

WEDNESDAY WAS PHIL'S DAY OFF. He planned to spend it at Monterey Bay pier, grubbing around the marina, maybe having lunch at the chili bar at the Cannery and visiting the new marine museum. He was dressed in cutoff jeans, an old blue sweatshirt, and a naval officer's cap, complete with shiny bill and gold braid. He fed Moe, who was squawking his head off, then headed toward his Jeep. The phone rang before he got out the door.

The matron at the jail sounded apologetic. Shannon wanted to see him.

He listened patiently, but he definitely didn't want to see Shannon. He told himself that twice. Then he climbed in the Jeep, cursed at himself, and headed for the county jail.

She'd been in custody for only a few days, but when Shannon entered the visiting room where he waited for her, he thought she looked thinner, more fragile. He held out his hand to shake, to let her know he wasn't angry about their last encounter, but she couldn't respond. Her hands were cuffed behind her.

"Hell," he snapped, storming out of the room. "Guard, come here and get those damned cuffs off of her."

"They're precautionary, Phil," the guard told him. "The last time you were here she came at you—"

Phil was adamant. "I said, take them off."

Shannon looked embarrassed as the cuffs were removed. "Thank you, Mr. Tewkes," she said, her voice barely audible.

"When I'm dressed like this, you can call me Phil."

A hint of a smile played at her mouth. "I like the hat," she said.

He grinned despite himself. "Me too," he said. "Why did you ask to see me, Shannon?"

She hesitated. "Can we sit down, please? There are several things—important things—I want to tell you."

He shook his head. "I'm no longer on your case. There's nothing I can do to help you, but the public defender—"

"No! Miss Taylor thinks I'm crazy. She wanted me to plead not guilty by reason of insanity. But I'm not guilty, and I'm not insane—and you have to help me prove it."

"Shannon, I'm telling you, I'm not involved in any way."

"But you're the only person I've talked to since I was arrested who actually paid any attention to what I was saying."

She stared straight at him, her eyes wide and clear. "I know you're not on my case, Mr.— Phil, but I hope you're still willing to be my friend." She was intense, but she was asking, not pleading.

He walked to the far side of the table and slumped into a chair. He'd listen to her, but he wasn't enjoying the prospect.

Sitting down across from him, Shannon folded her hands on the scarred wooden table as if she were an obedient schoolgirl. She paused, obviously collecting herself, then plunged in. "At first, I was too upset to think clearly, but these past two days I've gone over everything that's happened. Phil, I'm sure that James Johnson—you remember, the man I told you about who offered me a job in Los Angeles? Well, I'm convinced he's behind all this. That death certificate is a lie. It really is—and Mr. Johnson is the only person in the world who could have given the information that's on it."

Wondering why he'd come, Phil asked wearily, "What information are you talking about?"

"Several things," she said, leaning toward him eagerly. "First of all, my name. On the death certificate it's given as Shannon

Knight. I used that name only once in my life. I told Mr. Johnson my name was Shannon Knight—not Shannon Buchanan—because I thought it would make a better impression if Mandy and I had the same last name."

"Shannon, you've used so many different names—"

"And that's not all," she continued, unmindful of his interruption. "It says the mother's birthplace was Detroit, Michigan. I grew up near Detroit, but I wasn't born there. I was born in the northern part of the state in a little town called . . ." She hesitated for a moment. "I was born in a town called Pigeon."

"Pigeon, Mich," he echoed. "That's a good one. Not up to Valeria Valentine though." He paused. "But now that I think about it, on Mandy's birth certificate it says you were born in Daytona Beach, Florida."

She looked embarrassed. "Pigeon is such a dumb name. I didn't want it on Mandy's records, so I said Daytona Beach because that's where I got pregnant."

Phil waved his arm in an aimless gesture. "Almost the identical thing."

"No, it's not," she said, hanging her head. "And from now on I'm always going to tell the truth—"

"Not a bad idea," he interjected.

"But don't you see," she said, brightening. "Mr. Johnson is the only person who would think I was born in Detroit—I guess I wanted him to think I was from a big city. He asked me loads of questions, and I thought he was trying to find out if I'd be suitable for the job."

Phil ran what she was telling him through his mind. "Do you have anything else?" he asked.

"Yes! You told me the APB that was put out on me and Mandy—said I'd be in the Los Angeles area."

Remembering, Phil nodded.

She leaned farther across the table. "Phil, if I hadn't had car trouble, that's where I would have been. That's where Mr. Johnson expected me to be."

Before he could respond, she continued, "He knew I didn't have any relatives or people to help me prove Mandy was mine."

"Assuming he could have filed a fraudulent death certificate, why would he do it? Why would he want to frame you?"

Her eagerness deserted her. "I . . . I don't know. I've thought about that, too, but nothing makes sense."

"Shannon, you can tell Rita Taylor to ask the court to order blood tests when you go up for your preliminary hearing. If Mandy really is yours, blood tests will prove it and—"

"No! The tests *won't* prove it! Miss Taylor brought me a medical book with a whole chapter on blood tests. At first I couldn't understand it, but I read it over until I could."

She took a piece of paper from the patch pocket on her skirt. Reading it, she explained, "Blood tests for parentage used to be simple. They'd just compare what they call the antigen factors, A and B. The tests couldn't prove who *was* a parent, only who wasn't. And if you weren't just testing for paternity—if you were uncertain of a mother too—chances were pretty good you couldn't disprove a couple could be the parents of a particular child."

He nodded toward the notes she read from. "I'm impressed," he said, meaning it.

She looked up, a little smile on her face. "That's just the beginning. There's another blood test now called HLA. It takes a long time to complete. First they have to grow white blood cells —I can't understand that part—and then it takes a long time because there are so many possible combinations to check—but that's the point. The test can prove if a child *does* belong to a particular couple."

She looked at him. "That test can prove the Marshes are not Mandy's parents. But everyone believes that death certificate, and unless her father is tested, too, the test can't prove I'm her mother. I don't even know where her father is . . . and that's why you have to go to Texas."

"Why I have to do *what*?"

"Miss Taylor called Texas, but Ray Bob told her he could hardly remember me and that, for all he knew, it wasn't Mandy that I brought back with me. He was lying just because I never let him get his paws on me and—"

"Whoa! Who's Ray Bob?" Phil asked. Instinctively, he reached for his notepad, surprised to find himself patting the pocketless chest of his sweatshirt.

Going to the door, he called to the guard. "Bring me some paper and a pen, will you?"

Accepting a pad and pencil, he returned to Shannon and seated himself, instantly businesslike. "Now, from the beginning. You're going to tell me absolutely everything—from the day you left Arkansas to the day you got to Texas to the moment you arrived in California."

Shannon leaned toward him, her eyes luminous. She seemed to sit taller. "Thank you."

Two hours later Phil left the jail and headed for Monterey Bay, determined to salvage some of his plans for his day off. He walked around the marina, ate some chili, and stared out to sea. Not for a moment could he fool himself into thinking he was having a good time.

He watched the waves breaking against the pier. The evidence was stacked against Shannon, but she had raised some interesting points. Her grasp of the principles of HLA blood testing impressed him. She certainly didn't sound like a crazy who could have stolen another woman's child, and she was a lot smarter than he'd taken her for. And why would she be trying to come up with real evidence if she were guilty?

Despite himself, he felt personally involved. After all, who had handed the little girl over to the Marshes? And that was another thing. He had felt something when he was with them. A lack of conviction? A lack of joy? He had never been sure, but he'd sensed a reserve, a hesitation. And Patty Marsh hadn't been able to make a positive ID of Shannon as the kidnapper.

He kicked at the pilings, sending splinters of rotting wood into the swirling sea. He could talk to Taylor, find out what she'd learned, but he knew he would not be satisfied. Well, what the hell? He had vacation time coming. He looked out over the water.

Dumas, Texas? He muttered to himself. He'd have to be out of his mind. . . .

Rita Taylor was in court on Thursday morning. It was after lunch before Phil reached her. "Rita," he said, "Phil Tewkes. How are you?"

"Fine, I guess, Phil. Busy."

"Well, this won't take long. I talked to Buchanan yesterday. She—well, she thinks you don't have much faith in what she told you."

Taylor paused. "She's right. I don't have much reason to believe her. But I'm being paid to defend her, Phil, and I'll do the best I can. I'm going to ask the court for a psychiatric evaluation. I think that will be her best defense."

"A psychiatric evaluation."

"I'm not sure she knows the difference between fact and fantasy."

"I see," Phil said, his hackles rising at Rita Taylor's assertion. Despite the fact that Shannon had lied about her names, he felt she was basically honest. "She told me her version of what happened in Texas. I assume she told you too."

"Yes, she did. And I called Ray Bob Burke. His version is very different. According to him, she moved in with his mother because she had no place else to go. She stayed until it suited her to move on and then she went to L.A. And when she came back—this is important—he said they knew she was in trouble. They didn't realize what the trouble was, but he said she was always a good liar."

Phil grimaced. A good liar. Good enough to fool him?

"Listen, Phil, I have to get back to court. But I haven't seen you in ages. What about lunch tomorrow? Say Haddigan's, whatever time is good for you."

Phil noted the warmth in her voice. He visualized her: tall, not bad-looking. "Sure," he responded. "Tomorrow's fine. Meet you at one o'clock."

"Good, Phil, I'll look forward to it."

It didn't bother him to hear the smile in her voice.

❧ 13 ❧

Rita ordered white zinfandel, scanned the menu quickly, then removed her glasses and smiled across the table at Phil. "This was a lovely idea, Phil. We should have done it long ago."

Half nodding, Phil looked around. Haddigan's was an expensive fish house with a hewn-timber interior, leaded glass windows, and linen-covered tables. "You're right, Rita. It makes me feel important to think I can afford to be here."

She laughed. "Another time we can do something cheaper. Maybe I'll even cook for you."

He grinned. It was an open invitation. "I'll bring the zinfandel."

The waiter came to take their order. She asked for orange roughy, and he followed suit. "Sounds good to me."

He leaned back. Maybe it was time to satisfy his curiosity. "So—what's the story about Buchanan?"

"What about Buchanan? You have to know the DA has a solid case. The only question is whether she'll do hard time or walk on sympathy. So far, at least, she won't listen to my advice to plead insanity."

"Insanity," he repeated. "So you're discounting"—he chose his words carefully—"the possibility that she might be telling the truth?"

She raised an eyebrow. "The truth is, Buchanan's child is dead. I told you I talked to Ray Bob Burke, but it was only to appease Buchanan. He didn't ask why I was calling, and I didn't tell him, not that it would have mattered. Nothing he could have said would have made any difference. Phil, the woman is crazy."

"Maybe." He stabbed at the fish the waiter had set in front of him. "But she talks a good story."

Rita's laughter was derisive. "You can't be serious, Phil."

The fish didn't taste as good as he'd expected. "For her lawyer, you're giving her short shrift."

"Pardon me," she said, dripping sweetness. "For a cop, you're sitting on your brains."

He didn't respond, and he didn't respond later when she asked when he wanted to bring the zinfandel.

Phil was glad to get back to his Jeep. The public defender had made her position clear, and it annoyed him. If Shannon was ever to get any help, it wouldn't be from her.

He pulled into a parking spot at the sheriff's substation in Monterey, and after checking his message box, he took the small sheaf of memos and headed for his desk. He flipped through them quickly, discarded a few, and drew out one that caught his interest.

> *Phil, the address you told me to check in L.A. is in the middle of Forest Lawn Cemetery. Are you sure you had the number right or is the suspect a stiff?* NJG

The address Phil had asked the clerk to check was the one Shannon had given him—the place where James Johnson had told her she would have a job. Something else jarred his memory. The anonymous tipper had said he'd seen her near Santa Barbara and that she'd been headed toward L.A. *But she hadn't been anywhere near Santa Barbara.*

"Nancy," he said, picking up the phone and dialing an extension, "this is Phil Tewkes. Thanks for checking that address. Would you do one other thing for me? The APB on Shannon Buchanan

—find out where it originated. In fact, I'd like to see a copy. How fast can I have it?"

It was only minutes before the clerk brought it to him. Phil scanned the computer printout. The tipster had suggested the suspect would be in L.A.—but Vaughn had picked her up in the Bay Area. *And Shannon would have passed through Santa Barbara and been in L.A.—looking for the phony address James Johnson had given her— except for the last-minute car trouble that kept her in the Bay Area.*

Rita Taylor suspected that Shannon lied almost as easily as she breathed. But so far, Phil reflected, everything she'd told him had had a basis in fact—except for her collection of names. He rose from his chair and went to see Charlie Lawler.

The investigative sergeant was not receptive to Phil's request for time off. "If it isn't an emergency, we've got plenty to do here. Can't it wait a few weeks?"

Phil told him it couldn't. "There's something I need to do. It shouldn't take more than a few days."

Reluctantly, Lawler approved the request. "Back by the middle of next week?"

Phil nodded. When he got back he'd know one way or the other. Either Shannon was lying or she'd been framed.

Dumas, Texas. He shook his head. Vacation spot of the world . . .

Dumas, Shannon thought, sketching the feed store from memory, had been alternately scorching or freezing. But it had been good to her and Mandy at a time when they had really been in need.

She shifted the sketch pad for better light, pleased with the effect of what she'd drawn. Had it not been for Ray Bob, she might not have given in to her urge to see California.

Suddenly, Shannon needed to stretch. She put aside the sketch pad and, rising from the cot, paced the cell and began to do some knee bends.

She had not heard any more from Phil Tewkes since she had

talked to him yesterday. She prayed he was going to Dumas, as she'd asked. She visualized him there, walking the streets of the dusty downtown section, talking to the people who knew her.

Not that she'd really made friends in Dumas. She and Miss Ida had kept to themselves. But folks had been friendly enough to her and Mandy. They would have no reason to lie. No matter what Ray Bob said or didn't say, there would be others who could vouch for her to Phil.

They would know that when she had returned to Dumas after Miss Ida got so sick, Mandy had been with her, not some other child. They would know that, they would tell Phil they knew. Even Ray Bob would have to agree. He was repulsive, but he wasn't stupid.

And Mandy's baby pictures. They were in Miss Ida's house. Surely, Phil would find them . . . if he went to Texas. *If he went to Texas. Please, God, let him go to Texas.*

It was a fifty-mile drive from the Amarillo airport to Dumas— flat wheat fields dotted with Caterpillar oil derricks, hot under a relentless afternoon sun. The rented Ford was air conditioned, but Phil kept the windows rolled down, conscious of the change in atmosphere from the California coast.

If he'd come on official business, he would have had to stop at the sheriff's office and go through the formality of requesting permission to conduct an investigation. He'd considered that and decided against it. This trip he was strictly a tourist—maybe Dumas's first.

He saw Burke's feed and grain store within minutes of driving past the "Welcome to Dumas" sign. It was a big store but rundown, a barnlike structure in need of paint. Phil had planned to check into a motel first, to shower away the dust that seemed to cling to him, but at the sight of the store, he changed his mind.

He parked in an unpaved lot to the side of the store, then got out and stretched. His plaid shirt stuck to his back. He was thirsty, but eager to find Ray Bob Burke.

After the bright sunlight, the store seemed dim. It was cluttered but well stocked, not only with piles of feed sacks, but also with tack. A handsome saddle was on display near the counter.

A man—fat, with the leathered look of someone who'd spent too much time in the sun—lounged behind the counter with a beer in his hand. He matched Shannon's description exactly, right down to the beer. As Phil approached the man squinted at him through heavy-lidded eyes. "Howdy," he drawled.

Nodding, Phil ambled toward him. "Always this hot here in June?"

"Mostly." He smiled. "We're used to it. Where y'all from?"

"California. I'm looking for Ray Bob Burke."

The man's stare intensified. "All the way from California to see Ray Bob. What about, mister?"

Phil noted the slight apprehension that flitted across the man's face. "You wouldn't happen to be Burke, would you?"

Discarding a beer can, the man popped the top of a fresh one. "Yeah, and who all wants to know?"

"My name's Phil Tewkes. Got another beer? It's a long drive from Amarillo."

Burke nodded. "Reckon." He pulled another beer from the ice chest and put it on the counter.

Phil popped the top, then took a long swallow. Then, nodding his thanks, he said, "Ray Bob, I'm a friend of Shannon Buchanan. You remember her, don't you?"

"Shannon? Sure. Pack of trouble she's in, taking some kid like that."

Phil felt disappointment wash over him. So Dumas wasn't so far from the mainstream that they wouldn't get local news from the West Coast. "How'd you hear about that?" he asked.

Burke took a swig of beer before he answered. "Lucy Chercot —she works in the doctor's office round the corner—she brung in a newspaper and showed me the article. All about how Shannon stole another kid when her Mandy died."

Burke shook his head. "Sure surprised me. Didn't ever realize it wasn't the same kid when she came back. Hell, she didn't need to steal a kid—could of had another one of her own." Grinning, he added, "Maybe one that looked just like me."

Phil wasted no more than a second reflecting that no woman in her right mind and not many crazies would want a child that looked like him. What was important was that Ray Bob had never suspected the child Shannon brought back with her was not her own Mandy. *Maybe, just maybe, this trip wasn't going to be a wild-goose chase.*

He chose his words carefully, but kept his manner casual. "So, when Shannon came back to Dumas, you figured the little girl she had with her was Mandy. Couldn't tell any difference. That about it?"

Ray Bob shrugged. "Never paid much attention to the kid. Until they're old enough to fill a bra, girls all look pretty much the same to me. The mommy, now, she'd stand out in a crowd, but she had a lot to learn about socializing and knowing how to be nice to a guy."

Phil brought him back to the point. "But when Shannon returned, you had no reason to believe the child she had with her wasn't Mandy."

"Hell, how was I to know? The kid she brought back with her jabbered as much as the other one. I guess Shannon managed to find herself another talker."

Phil leaned across the counter toward Ray Bob and, despite his resolve, he heard the intensity in his own voice. "Shannon said there were pictures of Mandy at your mother's house. Pictures of her from the time she was a baby until just before she left for California in May. I'd sure like to see those pictures if you don't mind."

Ray Bob drew back, the expression on his face suddenly grim. "What d'want to see those pictures for?"

"Shannon claims the child she brought back to Texas was her daughter. She thinks those pictures will help her prove it."

Ray Bob stiffened. "Pictures ain't gonna prove a thing. The kid she brought back wasn't Mandy—might've talked a lot the way Mandy did, but she wasn't Mandy. It said in the papers that Mandy died, do you hear? Mandy died, and no one can make me say any different. I see what you're up to, but it won't work."

Phil was startled. He had triggered something, touched a nerve where Ray Bob was sensitive. "Well," he said, fingering a tooled leather belt that hung next to the counter, "it's no big deal. But I would like to see them—the pictures, I mean, if you can find them."

Ray Bob turned his back on Phil and popped open another beer. "I don't remember no pictures, and anyway, the house is in probate. Don't guess anyone could get in there just now."

From years of conducting interrogations, Phil could tell when a witness had clammed up, and he knew he wasn't going to get any more information about Mandy from Ray Bob.

He shrugged. "As I said, it's no big deal." Finishing his beer, he tossed a dollar on the counter.

Outside, he stood, hands on hips, looking up and down the street. That morning on the plane his thoughts had lingered on the Amanda Knight death certificate. He'd all but convinced himself the whole trip was pointless, but he'd been thirty-five thousand feet in the air and unable to turn back. Now, after talking to Burke, he was invigorated and ready to tack his sails into the wind.

Ray Bob *had* accepted the child Shannon returned with as Mandy, but it seemed as if Burke *wanted* Mandy to be dead. He'd certainly backed off as soon as Phil's questions suggested she might still be alive.

Phil knew he had to talk to more people, and the question was where to start. Shannon had given him some names—store clerks and neighbors—but on a hunch Phil decided to start with the woman Burke had mentioned, Lucy Chercot, who he'd said worked in a nearby doctor's office.

He located a doctor's office in a sterile little block of a building. He was in luck. The receptionist's name badge read "Lucy."

She was a big woman, a match for Burke, and Phil decided the food in town must be good. He started to reach for his badge, then remembered he wasn't on official business. He'd take his chances just asking questions. "Howdy, ma'am. The name's Phil Tewkes. I wonder if you could help me with something."

She looked him over. "Reckon," she said. "You looking for a place to stay?"

Phil smiled. "Well, I guess I am. But I'd like to ask you something first."

Lucy beamed, making her heavy cheeks stand out like two red apples, and he had a hunch he had come upon the town gossip. "Did you know Shannon Buchanan, a young woman with a little girl who lived with Ida May Burke?"

The apples bobbed. "My, yes," she chortled. "Shannon used to bring Miss Ida here to see the doctor—that is until Miss Ida was in a wheelchair and the doctor started checking on her out at her place."

Phil nodded. "And the little girl. Did you see her often too?"

"Sure I did. From the time she was just a little mite. Guess I never did see Shannon without her. It's a terrible thing that happened."

"What do you mean?" Phil asked, wanting to hear her version.

"Well, Mandy died. It's in the Amarillo paper. Mandy died in Los Angeles, and Shannon stole another baby just like her and brought the stolen baby back here to Dumas. Hard to believe. It really is."

"Sure is," Phil agreed. "Did you ever suspect the child Shannon brought back with her wasn't the same one she left with? Was there anything different? Anything suspicious?"

Lucy hesitated. "You a friend of Shannon's?"

"Yes, I guess you could say that. She's in a pile of trouble, and I thought I might turn up something in Dumas that could help her."

Lucy seemed satisfied. "Well now, I have to tell you, I don't know if I can be much help. See, when she came back here, I never suspected anything. The little girl seemed pretty much the same to me. But after I saw the newspaper article, I got to thinking and—" She broke off to answer the telephone.

Phil had a few minutes to think. She hadn't noticed anything different, and a woman would be more likely to pay attention to a little kid, at least more likely to than a man like Burke.

Lucy finished booking an appointment, then turned back to Phil. Unfortunately, the interruption seemed to have given her time to think too. "No, Mr. Tewkes, once I got to thinking about it, I realized there were just too many things different about that little girl. Hard to say just what they were—but it was a different kid all right. Everybody in town agrees. It's just about all anybody is talking about right now, and plenty of people are admitting they'd had their suspicions at the time. . . ."

Inwardly, Phil sighed. "Thanks, Lucy. What about that place to stay?"

Lucy wrote an address on the back of a prescription blank. "It's just at the edge of town."

"Thanks again, Lucy. Nice to meet you." He walked back out into the heat. He would have to talk to more people, but maybe it was a wild-goose chase after all.

❧ 14 ❧

By the time Phil checked into the motel Lucy had recommended near the outskirts of Dumas, it was late. He flopped on top of the bed unshowered, uncertain whether he was more exhausted or more frustrated. He had talked to at least a dozen people, most of whom hadn't seen much of Shannon and Mandy after they returned from California because Shannon spent most of her time taking care of Miss Ida.

He'd found no one who'd had strong enough doubts about Mandy's identity to mention it to anyone else *before* the story broke in the papers, but there were plenty of people now, *after* the story broke, who seemed to remember doubts they'd had and kept to themselves.

A few people admitted they'd never suspected a thing, but that wasn't enough to take into court. He'd found no one willing to swear the child Shannon brought back was the same one she'd left with.

Useless. Frustrating. He pulled himself off the bed and headed into the shower. In the morning he'd drive back to Amarillo and wait for his plane.

The bed was comfortable and he was exhausted, but he couldn't fall asleep. He tossed and turned, telling himself he couldn't have expected anything different. Who would assert the child Shannon returned with was Mandy when Mandy was allegedly already dead?

Tossing, he tried to sleep, but one question plagued him. Why hadn't one of those suspicious people been suspicious enough to report it?

When he finally dozed off, he slept well, too well. It was late when he awoke. He had time to get dressed, eat, and drive back to Amarillo, but he certainly wouldn't have time to spare.

Driving out of town, he spotted a diner. He'd only snatched a sandwich for dinner the night before and he was famished. And this was chili country. He was ready for a bowl of the hottest with an order of tortillas on the side.

The wizened old chap who served him gave him a toothless grin. "Y'all order hot around here, young fella, y'all best be prepared for hot."

The first spoonful brought tears to Phil's eyes. The old man stared at him, grinning.

"I get your point," Phil sputtered, reaching for his water glass. "Hot damn, it sure is good."

The old man winked at him, satisfied, then went back and busied himself behind the counter. "Y'all are a little too early or else you could have a piece of my chocolate mousse pie. Won't be ready for a while though."

Phil looked around. The diner was hardly a place where he'd expect to find chocolate mousse pie on the menu—if there was a menu. He hadn't seen one, only a blackboard behind the counter. "You make chocolate mousse pie, do you?" he answered, amused.

"The best," the old man answered. "We may be off the beaten track a bit, young fella, but we're still in the twentieth century. Hell, everybody in town comes in on the days I make chocolate mousse pie."

"No kidding," Phil said, mopping up the last of his chili with a fat tortilla.

He started to take another bite, then looked up abruptly. "How about—Shannon Buchanan, old-timer? Young, blond lady—used to take care of Ida May Burke? She ever—"

"Shannon? Hell, yes, she did. She and that little girl. Used to come in here just about every Sunday for a piece of that pie, right up till the time they left. Well, then, they was gone for a long time, two months, three months, I'm not rightly sure just how long it was. But the day they come in here again, the little one—Mandy, she's called—runs over and climbs up on that seat right there to see if I have any chocolate mousse pie. Chocolate mouse pie she always called it."

Phil decided not to interrupt, but to let the old man tell his story at his own pace.

The old man shook his head. "Well, I didn't have any pie that day, and she starts bawling me out, saying I should have saved her a piece and saved one for her Shannon. Always said her Shannon, not her mamma or her mommy the way most kids do. But then, she was a whole lot different than most kids. Talk! Well, I tell you, I could talk to her just the way I'm talking to you. And she'd answer right back. I promised t'have mousse pie the next time she came in, and that satisfied her."

The old man shook his head, wiping his hands on a striped towel. "Folks around here, they read that story in the paper—the one about that little girl dyin'—and they hopped right on it just as if it was gospel. But I ask you. I ask you," the old man repeated, his voice agitated, "how could anyone teach a little kid to come in here and ask for my chocolate mousse pie? Couldn't be done."

Phil was silent, amazed at how things worked in the world. He'd cast out a line in a lazy arc and hauled in a ten-pound trout. "Couldn't be done," he whispered, echoing the old man's words. *The child was Mandy, Shannon's Mandy.*

Phil put his spoon down and reached across the counter to shake the old man's hand. "Phil Tewkes," he said. "I'm a sheriff's investigator from Monterey, California. But I'm not here on official business—only as a friend of Shannon's."

"C. B. van Cliver is the name, C. B. for Cyrus Bruce, but

everyone calls me Clive," the old man told him, taking Phil's out-stretched hand with a surprisingly strong grip.

Clive's memory for detail was superb, and Phil never doubted he knew exactly what he was talking about. He had liked the child, liked Shannon, and his descriptions of them were accurate. Here was a witness Phil could take to court if and when it came to that.

"I talked to Ray Bob Burke yesterday," Phil said. "At first he told me he'd never noticed anything different about Mandy either, then suddenly he started insisting Mandy was dead—seemed all cut up at the suggestion she might still be alive."

"S'no wonder," Clive answered, nodding his head vigorously. "After Miss Ida died, some gal from a lawyer's office in Amarilly came around trying to find out where Shannon'd hightailed it to. Some-thin' about the will—Shannon and Mandy was named in it. Don't rightly know if Shannon knows about it, but Ray Bob sure does. S'pect he thinks if Mandy's dead and Shannon's locked up in the po-key for a good long while, he'll get their share. As 'tis now, he did get the store—which, frankly, mister, is more than he deserved."

Phil glanced at his watch. "Do you have a phone I could use? I have to call the airport in Amarillo."

He'd need to spend one more night in the vacation spot of the world. He would reschedule his flight for the following day.

It wasn't difficult to find Ida Burke's lawyer. Clive told Phil where Miss Ida had banked, and the bank manager, a squat little man who looked too young for the job, came up with the lawyer's business card pronto.

Phil telephoned and, wonder of wonders, found the lawyer in his office—a man by the name of Garrett Earl, who readily agreed to see Phil when he said he was a friend of Shannon's.

Driving to Dumas, he had felt tentative, but he didn't feel tentative now, and the road back to Amarillo seemed longer than it had the day before. It was past two when he reached the down-town area and found Garrett Earl's office. The heat was oppressive and Phil was thirsty, but he headed straight inside.

Earl was a portly old man with curly white hair. The sleeves of his white shirt were rolled up, and he sported a bolo tie fastened with the biggest chunk of raw turquoise Phil had ever seen. He sat behind a huge, dark wood desk, and he waved Phil to a seat.

"Howdy," he said with a drawl so deep Phil would not have been surprised to learn the man's horse was tethered at the back door. But the old man got right to the point. "Shame about that Shannon gal. Looked all over for her, and when she turns up, it's in a California slammer."

"I understand you were looking for her because she was mentioned in Ida May Burke's will."

"That's right." Earl leaned back in his chair. "And what's your interest, young fella?"

Despite Earl's rustic manner, Phil sensed he was dealing with a canny lawyer. He'd have to play it straight. Reaching into his back pocket, he took out his identification. "I have to tell you," he said, handing it to Earl, "I'm not here on official business. But I have been involved in the Buchanan investigation, and I'm in Texas trying to tie up a few loose ends."

Earl smiled, seeming to size Phil up. "All the way to Texas on your own. Can we rightly believe what we read in the paper? Or do you have ideas of your own?"

"I have ideas that Buchanan may be innocent, but that's beside the point."

Earl's eyes twinkled. "Not if the child they're disputing is really Amanda Knight, because if she is, she's coming into a legacy. So is Buchanan, for that matter. Miss Ida thought highly of them."

Phil leaned forward, surprised that Earl was even allowing for the possibility that Mandy was alive. "Did you know Shannon and Mandy? Did you see Mandy after Shannon came back from California?"

Earl shook his head. "Never laid eyes on either one of them in my life. But Ida May Burke sure did. She put a lot of stock in Shannon, and she loved that little tyke." He spread his hands behind his head. "Since I read about that death certificate, I've surely been bamboozled. Can't figure out why Ida May didn't realize it was a different child—unless, of course, as you're suggestin'—she wasn't."

"That's precisely what I'm suggesting, Mr. Earl—"

"Garrett," the lawyer said. "We ain't formal here."

Phil smiled. "Garrett, then. Yes, that's what I hope to prove."

"And Shannon's in the pokey." His eyes twinkled again. "Don't suppose she made bail."

"The bail is high—a hundred thousand dollars. She couldn't come up with ten percent." Phil paused. "If you knew where she was, why didn't you alert us about the legacy?"

"Hold on, young man." Garrett rose from his chair. "I was just getting to that. Dictated a letter to your public defender's office just a couple days ago. Let me look in this file, see if there's a copy. Faye —my secretary—she's gettin' old. Don't know if she sent it off yet."

He poked around on an old, wooden desk and came up with what he was looking for. "Yep, here it is. Darn that Faye. I'll see she gets it out in the mornin'."

"How much is the legacy?" Phil asked.

"Enough to make that bail and then some. Close to fifty thousand. Plus the house in Dumas," Garrett said. "All she left Ray Bob, her son, was the store."

Phil grinned to himself, knowing in that moment that he would have liked Ida May. "One more thing," he said. "Is that money tied up or can some of it be transferred to Monterey?"

"Won't be free and clear for a couple more weeks, but I don't see any problem, under extenuatin' circumstances, to advancing part of it now. You leave me the name of a Monterey bank and I'll see Judge Whitley tomorrow."

Phil got up to leave and reached across the desk to shake hands with Garrett Earl. The lawyer rose and came around his desk. "Glad you came by." He clapped Phil heartily on the back. "You take good care of that gal, now."

Phil tapped the chunk of turquoise in Earl's tie. "That's one hell of a spiffy rock."

❄ *15* ❄

EARLY WEDNESDAY MORNING, when Phil Tewkes boarded a plane in Amarillo, he knew every minute of his time in Texas had been worthwhile. He couldn't make a case with chocolate mousse pie, but Shannon was telling the truth. The child in San Diego was Amanda Desiree Knight, and he was going to prove it. He would start by doing a thorough investigation of the death certificate in Los Angeles.

Fastening his safety belt, he stretched his legs as far as the seat in front of him would allow, feeling very expansive. Texas had had an effect. He settled into his seat, grateful to have the few hours of flight time to think things over.

It was still hard to believe what Garrett Earl had told him—that between the house and bank deposits, Shannon and Mandy shared an inheritance of more than fifty thousand dollars. Phil grinned to himself, thinking about it. Fifty thousand dollars wasn't a fortune to most people these days, but what a mountain of money it would seem like to a woman who made her living doing portraits at two bucks a crack. Phil did some arithmetic. At two dollars a portrait, twelve portraits a day, fifty thousand dollars represented more than five years work without a day off.

And fifty thousand dollars would buy a lot of beers for Ray

Bob. Shannon was convinced her mysterious James Johnson had engineered a conspiracy to get Mandy away from her. If she was right, could Ray Bob be behind it? He certainly had a motive. If Shannon went to jail for kidnapping her own child, Ray Bob would—*no*, Phil rejected the whole idea. It was preposterous. Ray Bob wasn't bright enough to come up with a scheme to have Mandy falsely identified as a kidnapped child.

When the stewardess asked him to make a choice for lunch, Phil hardly heard her. He was totally absorbed, thinking about the death certificate. Could it really be fraudulent?

When Jack Avery, the reporter from the *Los Angeles Times*, had called to tell him about Amanda Knight's death, he had given Phil an accurate description of Shannon. What kind of odds would there be against a second Amanda Knight having a mother who looked just like Shannon? You'd get better odds trying to strike it rich playing the California lottery.

Phil stared at the tray the flight attendant put in front of him. He could eat, but food couldn't hold his attention. He would land at LAX at noon, and he would go to the Hall of Records—but first he wanted to talk to Jack Avery.

He called the *Times* from the airport. Identifying himself, he asked for Avery. The switchboard operator asked what department he was in.

"He's a reporter. I suppose that would be news or city news," Phil answered, glancing at his watch.

"News desk, Sanders speaking."

"Jack Avery, please."

"Avery? I don't think there's an Avery in this department, I'll put you back on the switchboard—"

"Hold it!" Phil shouted. "This is Inspector Phil Tewkes of the Monterey County sheriff's office. And if you don't know a Jack Avery, I want to talk to your editor."

Minutes later, Phil hung up, but he still held the receiver tight in his hand. *There was no staff reporter named Jack Avery. The editor said there never had been, not in all the years he'd worked for the paper.*

Collecting himself, he ran out of the terminal and pushed ahead of a man who was headed for the lead taxi. "Excuse me, police," he said. The man probably didn't believe him, but Phil didn't care. He had to get to the Hall of Records.

It was a quarter to two when he shoved some bills into the taxi driver's hand and bolted toward the County Building. Inside, he felt as if he was running through a maze to hunt down a hunk of cheese, but finally he found the office he was looking for.

Showing a clerk his identification, he explained that he needed to examine a death certificate.

When he gave her the name and number, she nodded. "We'll call it up for you on microfiche."

In an amazingly short time he was staring at Amanda Desiree Knight's death certificate displayed on a computer screen. "Born in Little Rock, Arkansas, on October 29, 1985, died Los Angeles, California on June 26, 1987. Mother's name, Shannon Knight."

For a moment the official document in front of him shook his conviction that Mandy was still alive. But he'd first heard about this death certificate from Jack Avery—and there was no Jack Avery.

Phil called the clerk. "Look at this death certificate carefully, please. Is there anything unusual about it?"

"Unusual? What do you mean? It looks okay to me."

"I asked you to look closely. Examine the seal and—"

She interrupted. "There's nothing wrong with it. I see hundreds of these come through here every month, and I don't see anything irregular about this one."

Phil continued to stare at the computer screen, willing it to give him a clue. It had been filed from County-U.S.C. Medical Center—just as the nonexistent Jack Avery had said.

County-U.S.C. Medical Center. Maybe that would be a blind alley, too, but he was going to check it out.

It was a fifteen-minute cab ride east on the San Bernardino Freeway to County-U.S.C., a sprawling complex behind graffiti-covered walls in the midst of East Los Angeles.

Phil had the driver take him to Admitting. He thrust a ten-dollar bill at the man, then sprinted across the concrete driveway without waiting for change.

Inside, the place was teeming with humanity, a polyglot of ethnic types having trouble making themselves understood in anything but their native tongues. A feeling of frustration was palpable in the air, but he put aside his sense of decorum and pushed to the head of the line.

"Phil Tewkes, sheriff's investigator," he told a harried-looking clerk, allowing her only a quick glance at his ID in the hope she wouldn't catch its place of origin. "I need to see the admittance record for Amanda Desiree Knight. She would have been admitted sometime near the end of June 1987—"

The clerk spoke without looking up. "Sorry, admittance records a year old aren't in this department."

"Where are they, then?"

"On microfilm."

"Where?"

The clerk gestured behind her.

Phil watched the sullen, dark-haired young woman continue filling out a form. Then he put his hand on hers, forcing her to look up. "I need those records, and I need them now. Can you go and get them?"

The clerk jerked her hand away. "Look around. How do you suggest I leave this front desk?"

"I really don't care. This is important. Who is your supervisor?"

The clerk met his gaze for the first time, seemed to measure his authority. She grimaced. "Give me a minute, will you?"

"A minute's all I've got."

He leaned on one elbow, drumming his fingers on the counter-top until the woman returned.

"Knight? K-n-i-g-h-t?" she asked, spelling it out.

"That's it. Amanda Knight."

The clerk shook her head. "Wasn't admitted. There's no record of an Amanda Knight being admitted last June."

Phil blinked. "The last two weeks of June? Look again. Her death certificate was filed out of this hospital."

The young woman put her hands on her hips. "Look, I told you there's no record of admittance. You can see my superior if you want. Nadine Williams, down that hall on your left. It won't do you any good."

Phil glanced over his shoulder as he hurried down the hall. "You're wrong," he called. "It might be exactly what I want."

Phil knocked but swung the door to the office open with the same motion. The woman behind the desk with the nameplate "Nadine Williams" was studiously filing her nails. Again, he whipped out his identification, flashed it in front of her, then slipped it back in his pocket. "The clerk out front can't find a record of an admittance in June 1987. Will you check for me, please? It's very urgent. I need those records for an investigation."

Nadine Williams opened a drawer and dropped her nail file inside. "Name?" she asked.

Phil said the name slowly. "Amanda Desiree Knight." Then he added, "She was a small child. She would have been a pediatrics patient."

Phil watched her sashay out. Waiting, he glanced at his watch, but she returned in less than ten minutes.

"Sorry," she said. "It isn't there. No one admitted by that name." She anticipated his next request. "I checked the weeks before and after. I find no record of an Amanda Knight being admitted to this hospital."

No record of an Amanda Knight. Phil closed his eyes and let it sink in with stunning finality, then he looked at the woman facing him. "How could a death certificate bearing her name have been filed from this hospital on June 26?"

Nadine Williams shrugged. "I have no idea."

"Then suppose you do some more checking. I'd like to see a list of all death certificates filed from this hospital during June."

"I don't believe there is any list like that. The certificates are filed routinely. The information is taken directly from the patient's chart, the form is filled out, and then sent downtown."

Nadine Williams stared at him defiantly. "You can check that out if you want. Every floor has its own records clerk who handles the outgoing forms. But if there was no admittance, then there was no patient, so how could anyone file a death certificate?"

Phil nodded. "Good question. That's what I want to know."

He pondered a minute. "Tell me—exactly how difficult would it be for someone to file a false certificate?"

Nadine's round face reflected bafflement, then she shrugged again. "I don't guess it would be too difficult—not really—now that I think it over. The forms are on every floor. Anybody could get one. If they filled it out and scrawled in a doctor's signature, I guess they could just bury it in a stack of legitimate ones and send it on downtown."

She smiled at Phil for the first time. "Hey, that would make a great movie! Somebody files a fake death certificate and . . . wham! Some guy is considered dead! I wonder if anybody ever thought of that. . . ."

"Somebody did," Phil said. "Nadine, you've been a lot of help. But I have one more question. I presume those blank forms come in by the stack and are distributed on every floor."

"Sure," she agreed. "They aren't dated until they're used, if that's what you're getting at."

"That's exactly what I'm getting at," Phil murmured. "Nadine, you're a peach. Thanks a lot." He waved at her as he turned to go.

With rising excitement, he strode down the hall and made his way to the door. Anybody could have filed that certificate. James Johnson could have access to this hospital—possibly through someone else. More important, he had proof now that Shannon had been framed—the whole case was a frame.

He looked for a cab, didn't see one, and sprinted to the front of the building.

The death certificate forms were numbered when printed but dated only when used. The form used to file Amanda Knight's had to have been taken from the stack in sequence. But if Phil was right—if James Johnson, or anyone else, had used that form to file Mandy's death certificate, it would have been only in the last few weeks—*after* Johnson's encounter with Shannon by the side of the road in Monterey. And the claimed date of death, June 26, 1987, would not match up with the dates on that particular sequence of numbered forms.

Spotting a cab, Phil whistled through his teeth, and the driver pulled toward the curb. Phil glanced at his watch. Four-forty. He hopped into the back seat. "Hall of Records, downtown," he ordered tersely. "An extra five if you make it in ten minutes."

The cab driver didn't earn the extra five. They got tied up in traffic on the freeway interchange. At five to five, Phil leaned back in the cab. "Forget it. What's a decent hotel around here?"

The cab driver took him to a downtown hotel—a round, silver bullet of a building with glass-encased elevators on the outside.

Phil whistled. "What's the tariff on a place like this?"

The cabbie shrugged. "A hundred ten, maybe twenty, a night. You want this or some place cheaper where you have to bring your own roach powder?"

Phil took another look at the hotel. He had sixteen hours to kill. He hadn't had a vacation in years—unless he counted Dumas. It was doubtful he'd get any reimbursement from the sheriff's department, but what the hell. He'd earned this, and anyway—he didn't want to spend sixteen hours waging war against an insect population.

His canvas overnight bag didn't look like Gucci, and the man at the registration desk looked at him doubtfully.

"I'll pay in cash. One night only," Phil told him. Then he added, "And I want a decent view."

He followed the bellboy into the glass elevator, and riding up, he tried not to act like a tourist, ogling the panorama. The room was smaller than he'd expected, but luxurious, with deep carpets, crystal light fixtures, a marble bathroom—and the biggest bed he'd ever seen. Phil grinned wryly. *What a waste.* He looked for the room-service menu.

A cola cost $3.50—forget the rest of it. He guessed he'd go downstairs—find someplace else to have dinner. As he showered

and shaved in the marble bathroom, he couldn't help musing that
Theresa Ames would love every bit of the opulence—and that
Shannon would be absolutely awed.

The weather was right for walking, he decided, stepping out
of the hushed elegance of the hotel.

He walked for blocks, fascinated at the seediness of the downtown area that surrounded the silver bullet. He found himself across
the street from Parker Center, the publicized hub of the Los Angeles
Police Department, and he wondered briefly what his life would
be like if he'd chosen to spend it as a big city cop instead of on a
bluff in Monterey.

The thought was disturbing, and he didn't want to do any heavy
pondering, especially on an empty stomach. He spotted a narrow
storefront, the gloomy facade of a diner, and loping across the street,
he went inside. It was smoky and too warm, but he sat down at a
rickety wooden table and ordered a ham and cheese on rye and a
beer.

Three guys—in their early twenties, maybe—huddled at one
end of the counter. After a few minutes, Phil realized they were
almost taking turns checking him out. Careful not to glance in their
direction, he took another bite of sandwich and held up his empty
beer bottle to signal the man behind the counter to bring him
another.

He wondered if he had *cop* written all over him—if they could
tell just by looking at him that there was a badge in his pocket. He
sank his teeth into the second half of his sandwich. Either that, or
they thought he might have some bucks in his pocket. A candidate
for a mugging.

Suddenly, he was struggling against the urge to laugh out loud.
What the hell was he doing? From the ritz to the pits—he didn't
belong in that elegant hotel, and he didn't belong in a sleazy diner.
That's probably why the guys at the counter were so alert. Something was wrong. He was out of place.

He took a long drink of the second beer. The damn thing was,
he wasn't sure where he did belong. He thought about that big

bed—or, worse yet, the bed at home, much smaller of course, but more than big enough because he could sleep in the middle.

The urge to laugh was gone now.

Maybe, he pondered, if Theresa hadn't had her heart set on a career in television . . . or maybe if she hadn't been so successful . . . For a moment he imagined the svelte Terry Ames in a gingham dress, welcoming him home after a hard day.

He jerked to his feet and threw enough money to cover the tab on the table. Two beers, he told himself, only two beers. God, he'd make a maudlin drunk.

He headed back to the hotel. He was certainly paying enough for the privilege of staying there, and he was going to enjoy it if it killed him.

❧ 16 ❧

DRESSING THE NEXT MORNING, Phil knew that he had a decision to make. He was not in his jurisdiction. Without the consent of the Los Angeles Police Department he had no legal right to be conducting an investigation here.

He could call Lawler, with luck get ahold of him right away, and have him initiate a courtesy request to the LAPD allowing Phil to pursue his investigation. It could take hours, though, before permission came through.

On the other hand, Phil told himself, he was not interrogating any witnesses—not examining a crime scene. In fact, maybe all he was doing was what he should have done before he sent that kid home with the Marshes. He knew he was rationalizing, but his decision was made by the time he arrived at the Hall of Records. Oh hell, he was a good cop and believed in the rules, but he was here already.

This time he bypassed the clerk and went right to the supervisor—a prim, older woman who reminded him of his sixth-grade teacher, Beulah Paul.

"Yesterday I saw a death certificate on file here—for a little girl named Amanda Knight. It was filed at County-U.S.C. Medical

Center on June 26, 1987. But the hospital has no record of a patient named Amanda Knight, dead or alive."

Beulah Paul's double looked haughty. "Then I would say County-U.S.C. Medical Center doesn't keep accurate records."

Phil smiled, trying for the same boyish grin he knew had always gotten to Miss Paul. "The accuracy of their records isn't what's important here," he said. "What may be important is that the alleged date of death filed on that certificate may not match up with other deaths recorded on certificates in that numbered sequence."

His grin had obviously not impressed her. She stared at him coldly. "We have nothing to do with the sequence of numbers on blank forms received by each hospital. All we record is the information on them when they come back to us."

"Look," Phil said, wanting to appeal to the woman's sense of order, "I'm going to ask you to do something—just to be sure that the death certificate you have on file for Amanda Knight has not been tampered with somehow."

"Young man," the woman began, making Phil realize he had not bothered to identify himself, "what exactly do you want me to do?"

"Ma'am, I realize it's time-consuming, but this really is important. There could be a legacy at stake here. What I'd like you to do is check the dates of death recorded on certificates numbered, say, twenty back and twenty after the number on Amanda Knight's." He spoke quickly, trying to make himself look earnest. "Ma'am, I would really appreciate that."

This time he seemed to have struck a chord with Beulah's look-alike. Her mouth quivered as she deliberated.

"A legacy, you say?"

"Yes, ma'am, a nice-sized legacy that would help her grieving mother quite a bit."

He hoped he hadn't overdone it. There was some truth to the legacy.

The woman nodded slowly. "You realize this may take a while. It's really very irregular. I would say it will take at least an hour. Why don't you come back at ten?"

Phil nodded vigorously. "I will. I'll be back at ten. And thank you, ma'am, I appreciate your time." He turned and strode quickly out of the room before she could change her mind.

In the hallway, he chastised himself for putting on that little show—ingratiating himself with the supervisor. But he saw no reason to identify himself as a peace officer. All he wanted was the same kind of information any citizen might request. And a letter to that effect to take up to Lawler. Which reminded him, he thought, digging in his pockets for change, he needed to find a telephone.

"Nadine Williams," he said, reaching the hospital. He waited until she was on the line. "Nadine," he began. "This is Investigator Phil Tewkes. I was there yesterday. Do you remember?"

"Sure," she said. "You know I've been thinking a lot about that script about a fake death certificate—"

Phil cut her off. "Yeah, I know what you mean. It sure would be dramatic. Listen, Nadine, I need you to do something—and I'm leaving town in a couple of hours. I need you to write me a letter verifying the information you determined for me yesterday—that no patient named Amanda Knight was admitted to or died at County-U.S.C. Medical Center during the month of June 1987."

"A letter?" Nadine asked.

"Just something simple. I'll stop by and pick it up on my way to the airport."

"Oh," she said. "Yes, sure, I could do that. If you come around noon, I'll be free for lunch."

Phil grinned, but with any luck he would have no time to take her up on it. "Wish I could," he said. "I owe you one. But I honestly do have a plane to catch."

"Oh," she said again. "Well, that's too bad. I'll get the letter typed up right away."

He hung up and shoved his hands in his pockets. Nearly an hour to kill. And if Beulah's double turned up what he hoped, he would need a letter from her too. He checked a directory near the elevator, hoping to find a coffee shop. He had not taken time for coffee earlier, but he was ready for a cup now.

*　　*　　*

The supervisor was on her coffee break when Phil returned to her office. She returned a moment later, looking pleased with herself, and waved to Phil, asking him to follow her.

"You know," she said, "you were absolutely right. There is something wrong with this filing." She sounded breathy, like a co-conspirator. "Something is very, very wrong."

She explained exactly what Phil had hoped to hear—that dates of death filed on that sequence of numbered forms had been for June 1988. *June 1988—a full year after the date of death typed in on Amanda Knight's.*

Whoever had filed that fraudulent certificate had used forms currently in use—supposing, Phil thought, that no one would ever bother to check the form's legitimacy. He strained to read the signature of the attending physician. It was totally illegible. It was either a doctor with a handwriting even worse than most or else—and Phil was almost certain this was the case—the doctor didn't exist.

"I have one more question," he said to the supervisor. "Can you tell me when this certificate—the one for Amanda Knight—was actually filed?"

"Of course," she replied, looking smug. "It was filed about two weeks ago."

Two weeks ago. Phil was exultant. *About the time Shannon met James Johnson.*

So what if the woman looked like Miss Paul. After he got the letter he needed, he grabbed her and kissed her hard.

By the time he hailed a cab to LAX, with Nadine's letter added to the one already in his pocket, he had begun to put the thing together.

Now he knew what had happened. Someone with connections to County-U.S.C. Medical Center had filed the fraudulent death certificate. Phil had no doubts about that. What he didn't know was why. Was it only that someone had been out to frame Shannon? Or did that someone—James Johnson?—want to close the books on the kidnap of Suzanne Marsh by fooling them all into believing that Mandy was Suzanne?

The person who had fingered Shannon had said he had seen a poster of Suzanne Marsh and thought she was the child in Shannon's custody. Maybe, Phil pondered, that poster was the key. Maybe someone had been frightened by that poster and had thought Shannon and Mandy offered a way out.

He leaned back in the seat and closed his eyes. There was more to this case than he'd thought. He had the eerie premonition that there was more at stake here than proving Shannon's innocence— that when it was all over, she would have Mandy back and the real Suzanne would be found.

It was late Thursday afternoon when Phil reached home. He stopped only long enough to feed a loudly squawking Moe, then he headed for the county jail to see Shannon.

When she was led into the visiting room, Phil decided she had lost weight in the short time he had known her. Her large eyes, frightened and serious, looked larger than ever in the thinner face, but she smiled hopefully when she looked at him.

"Mr. Tewkes . . . Phil, did you talk to people in Dumas? Did they tell you that when I came back after I'd been in Los Angeles, my Mandy was the same child I'd left with?"

"Sit down, Shannon. We have a lot to talk about."

She perched on the edge of a chair, leaning toward him, her arms outstretched across the table. "Did they, Phil? Did they tell you it was always Mandy?"

He reached over and took her hand, squeezing it to steady her. "Most of the people in Dumas won't swear that the child you brought back with you from L.A. was the same Mandy you left with."

Her eyes filled with tears. "Oh, my God! That can't be. They'd have to know. They'd have to realize. I swear to you, she's my Mandy."

Phil squeezed her hand again. "People in Dumas had heard that

Mandy was dead and you had kidnapped another child, so it's understandable. If Mandy had died, they knew you couldn't have brought her back with you."

Pulling back from him, she covered her face with her hands, crying. "She didn't die. She didn't die."

"I know that, Shannon," he said, softly. "The child you were picked up with is Mandy, and I have all the proof we need."

With her hands still covering her face, she spread her fingers to stare at him. "You believe me, Phil? You know?"

He smiled at her. "The trip wasn't wasted. I came back convinced you were telling the truth, and now I've got plenty more to go on. And I've got other news too—news you're going to like."

The gratitude that shone in her face made Phil feel strangely embarrassed. "Tell me, Phil. Tell me everything. I am telling the truth, but how . . . what convinced you?"

"Chocolate mousse pie started it, Shannon. But that's not important now." He took a deep breath. "Shannon, Mandy's death certificate was filed just two weeks ago. It's a fraud—and there's no record of her having ever been a patient in the hospital where the certificate originated."

He noted how quickly she pulled herself together. She was alert and attentive to every word. "Then I'm right. There *is* a conspiracy to steal Mandy," she said firmly.

Phil shook his head. "I've gone over it carefully, and I'm pretty sure the real object of all this is to close the book on the Marsh case."

"Why? If the Marshes are behind it, they know Mandy isn't their daughter. So why would they—"

"The Marshes aren't behind it," he said, interrupting. "But I'm pretty sure that whoever is behind it knows where Suzanne Marsh is. Someone wants the case closed so that people will stop looking for her."

Shannon jumped up, suddenly jubilant. "Oh, I hope her parents get her back—but if the death certificate is a fraud, that proves Mandy is mine. You'll have to let me out of here and get Mandy back for me."

Phil stood up and put his hands on her shoulders. "You're right, but . . . well, I want to talk to you about something first." He sat her down again, watching her jubilance turn to apprehension.

"First of all," he told her, "you can get out of here on bail. We can—"

"Bail! Never! At my arraignment the judge set bail at one hundred thousand dollars. The public defender told me I'd only have to post ten percent—*only* ten thousand dollars. There's no way in the world for me to get that much money."

"Shannon, that's the other part of my good news. You already have that much money—and more. You and Mandy inherited about fifty thousand dollars in cash and property from Ida May Burke."

The news seemed to stun her. "Why . . . why would Miss Ida leave so much to us?"

"I suppose," he said, "because she cared about you." He paused. "I can understand that. She cared about Mandy too. She wanted to take care of the two of you."

"She . . . she was a very sweet old lady," Shannon told him with a choke in her voice. "And smart up to her last day. Ray Bob was her son, her only relative, but he didn't pay any attention to her. I guess I tried to make that up to her."

"Well, I'd say you did a good job and that she left you the money and house in gratitude. But the important thing right now is that I've seen her attorney in Amarillo. Now that he knows where you are, he's arranging to have a bank draft deposited for you in Monterey. Once it is, we can get you out of here—at least until your preliminary hearing."

"I'm glad about the money, of course I am, but why do I need to post bail? Why do I have to go to court at all? If you know Mandy's mine, can't the judge just drop the charges against me?"

Phil nodded. "He could, but, Shannon—there's something else for us to think about. I gave you the benefit of the doubt and went to Dumas. It's your turn to trust me."

Shannon stared at him, waiting.

"I'm convinced Suzanne Marsh is still alive, and she is someplace where she can be found—if people are looking for her."

"You said that, but—"

"Wait. Let me finish. If we go public, whoever is behind all this may panic and hide Suzanne where she'll never be found. Or something even worse could happen to her." His voice was grim, and her expression told him she'd caught his meaning.

"But . . . what can we do? I have to get Mandy back soon. She won't understand what happened to me. She's so little . . . she must be so afraid . . ."

He tried to soothe her. "For the moment, Mandy is being well taken care of, and there's no point in raising more publicity when you get out on bail. We'll have everything ready to get the case dismissed at the time of your preliminary hearing."

Shannon looked doubtful, but she listened quietly as Phil bent toward her. "We have to find out who filed that death certificate. Shannon, think carefully. Tell me absolutely everything you can remember about the man who called himself James Johnson."

She sat down again, and he pulled up his chair to sit beside her. "Think hard, and remember every question he asked. And describe him to me— No, don't describe him! Draw him. Do you remember what he looked like well enough to do that? Can you do a picture of him like the one you did of me?"

Shannon nodded. "I did two pictures of him already—he claimed one was for his mother." She winced. "But he asked me questions all the time I was sketching. I'll have to concentrate, but if you bring me some good chalks and medium-textured paper, I'll do a real portrait of him."

The fading rays of sunlight had dimmed into early evening before Phil left her. "We'll have you out of here by this time to-morrow," he told her, "and, meantime, I'll get you the chalks and paper."

❊ 17 ❊

NEELY SMITH SANK into the deep azure cushions of Lorelei Connelly's French provincial sofa, waiting for Roger. It was Thursday. There were only two days left before the charity fund-raising dinner in San Francisco Sunday night. Neely had everything under control, but he wanted to give Roger the details.

He stood as Lorelei entered the room. She was wearing a full-skirted, magenta lounging dress, and she seemed to pose in the doorway.

"Lorelei, you look absolutely breathtaking—as always."

"Thank you, Neely." She flashed a languid smile as she swept across the thick white carpet. "Roger will be home soon, but go ahead and fix us a drink."

Neely crossed to the oak-paneled bar that took up one wall of the room and set up two crystal glasses. "Coming up."

He poured Chivas Regal from a cut-glass decanter. "I think Roger will be pleased with the guest list for Sunday's fund-raiser," he told her. "The response has been even better than we'd hoped for."

"I'm sure he'll be pleased," she said, perching on a mauve settee. "He doesn't always show his appreciation, but I wonder how he could have gotten along without you this past year." She laughed, a soft, throaty sound. "Sometimes I'm almost jealous of the bond between you two. It makes me feel a little like an outsider."

Neely smiled as he handed her the drink. "It's not just this past year. Remember, Roger and I go back a long time."

Sipping the drink, she leaned back in the cushions. "Perfect. It's been a trying day." Suddenly, she grimaced and reached her free hand behind her. "What on earth—"

Neely watched her retrieve something from between the cushions. "Looks like a piece of china."

"My God, it's a piece of my Lladró figurine—the one Roger and I brought back from Acapulco." She jerked to her feet, spilling her drink. "I've told that child a million times to stay away from it. It was such a lovely piece—"

"Stay away from what?" Neely hadn't heard Roger cross the long Italian-tile entryway, but now he stood behind them.

"My Lladró, Roger. The one you bought for me. That child is simply incorrigible. She not only broke it, she tried to hide it."

"She's just a child, darling." Roger kissed her cheek. "Children have accidents, don't they?"

"Not if they listen and do as they're told—"

"Lorelei, you're always on her about something!"

Neely moved smoothly between them. "Now, now, you two, let's not argue about Kelly again. You're both right about her. She's an adorable kid, but she is full of mischief."

"Besides," Roger said, taking Lorelei's hands, "I'll tell you something much more important. Neely, fix me—fix me whatever it is you're having. My news is worthy of a toast."

As he poured the drink Neely watched Roger, glad to see him so exuberant. He handed him a glass and sat across from them. "We're ready. Let's hear your news."

Roger sipped. "You know that television interview we did the other morning? A lot of good repercussions, apparently—especially since that woman's been arraigned and the child's been sent home with her family."

Neely rose and walked back to the bar, speaking over his shoulder. "It looks as if that case is settled. There's no need even for blood tests."

He had to catch his breath, but he continued, casually. "Best of all, the timing was perfect for your campaign." He couldn't push the issue, but he needed to know exactly where Roger stood. Would the district attorney order the blood tests anyway or simply accept his good publicity and consider the case closed?

"Blood tests," Roger repeated, pensively. "Maybe you're right. Maybe we don't need them at this point. Personally, the Buchanan woman has my sympathy—not that I'd ever go public with that. But nothing is to be gained by dragging this out. I talked to Rita Taylor—the public defender on the case. Told her that if she could get Buchanan to enter a plea of not guilty by reason of insanity, we'd move fast. Get her into therapy as soon as possible."

Keeping his back to Roger, Neely took a gulp of his drink. He'd been nervous when the girl was picked up in the Bay Area instead of near Santa Barbara, where he'd reported seeing her. But no one in the media ever picked up on the discrepancy.

The possibility of blood tests had been the only other thing he hadn't been able to control. But Roger's interest in the case and his enthusiasm for closing it seemed to have eliminated that threat. Unknowingly, Roger was doing everything just as if Neely had written the script.

Flashing a smile, he turned back to face Roger. "I've got the guest list for the fund-raiser, but we can go over it later. Let's hear about these good repercussions."

Roger turned to his wife. "Pick something elegant and gubernatorial out of your closet, Lorelei. I got a call from the producers of the *California Today* show. They want us to do a television interview. They must have decided I've shaken what they called my playboy image and am good enough for them now."

Lorelei threw her arms around him. "Oh, Roger, that's wonderful."

Neely stood up and raised his glass. "You're on a roll, Rog. Everything is falling into place."

Roger nodded, turning serious. "According to the party bigwigs, I'll be doing more tomorrow than just taping an interview. I'll be giving the voters of California a look at their next governor. They need someone strong to run against the incumbent, and they think I'm their best shot. I hope they're right. From interim DA to governor is a big step." He shook his head, slowly. "I hope I'm ready."

Lorelei laughed. "You're ready for anything, darling. Neely, public relations is your forte. Any ideas about what I should wear?"

"Whatever you like," Neely said. "You'll be a vision whatever you choose."

"Do you really think so?" Lorelei jumped up. "Oh, Neely, what would we do without you?" Her voice grew intense. "You know, don't you, that you'll have to come with us to Sacramento?"

Neely glanced at Roger, then turned to Lorelei. "I never doubted it for a minute."

Patty Marsh took special pains with her appearance as she dressed for her talk at the benefit for Find the Children. She hadn't cared about cosmetics and hairstyles since Suzy was taken. Now, staring into the bathroom mirror, it startled her to see how attractive she still looked with a new hairdo and a little blusher and mascara. She smiled at her reflection, feeling good. Better than good. She felt wonderful.

Earlier that evening, just before they'd sat down to dinner, Daniel had grabbed her in a bear hug. "We've got our Suzy back, and I've got my Patty back. You're relaxed—you're your adorable, squeezable self again."

Laughing, she had turned up her face for his kiss. Yes, she was feeling better. Just today Suzy had started calling her Mommy. Daniel was Daddy to her, and Suzy and Danny Joe were playing together like brother and sister; they'd even argued over a toy. She had her family back. Truly. They were all together again.

Still studying herself in the mirror, she brushed her hair vigorously. She wanted to look her best, not just for Daniel and the audience, but for herself. She wanted to be the old Patty—the

Patty who always looked bright and fresh and who was naturally attentive to details.

She struggled with a rising feeling of nervousness, reminding herself how many times she had rehearsed her talk with Daniel. Then, slipping into a new blue and white print dress, she gave her lipstick one last touch-up and smiled again at her reflection.

Never give up hope. That was the one thing she would stress for other parents of missing children—that and the need for publicity. If it hadn't been for the Find the Children posters, Suzy might never have been recognized.

"Patty, are you ready?" Daniel called. "It's nearly seven o'clock and Mom's here."

Patty gave instructions to Stella. "They're both to be in bed by eight. They can have a snack before they brush their teeth—"

"Honey, I think it's time we get going . . ."

She took a deep breath. "I'm coming."

The community center was a cinder-block building in a park a few miles from their house. The parking lot was full.

Patty's mouth suddenly felt dry. "Daniel," she whispered, "I don't know—all those people. I'm so nervous."

Daniel smiled. "You'll do just fine. All those people are happy for us. You've gone over your talk a dozen times. You'll get up there and say what you have to say."

They were greeted with applause when they entered. Patty felt embarrassed, but glancing at Daniel, she saw him grinning broadly and waving his hand in acknowledgment.

A tall, stylish woman rushed up to them. "I'm Penny Stewart," she said. "I'm so glad to meet you, and I can't thank you enough for coming tonight. We're all delighted to have you. Before we get started, I want to introduce both of you to some of our members."

Patty let herself be led down an informal receiving line of people who pumped her hand and told her how happy they were for her and her family. It was hard to focus on faces, but the voices were warm and sincere. Patty found herself returning the firm grips and smiling. "Thank you. Thank you. You're all so kind."

Then Penny Stewart led them to seats in front of the assembly. "If you're ready, I think it's time we begin."

Patty nodded, almost eager, but she tensed a little as Penny introduced her. ". . . and now, it is my happy duty to introduce to you the parents of the recently recovered Suzanne Marsh, Daniel and Patty Marsh."

When the applause stopped, she beckoned to Patty. "As you all know, Mrs. Marsh is our speaker tonight."

Patty took a deep breath and mounted the stairs to the platform. She glanced quickly at the sea of eager faces, adults and a few children, then arranged her notes on the lectern. She had gone over her talk so often, she didn't really need the notes, but handling them in a businesslike fashion gave her a feeling of confidence.

Looking up, she smiled. "I want to thank all of you for your warm welcome and for the support this community gave to my family throughout our ordeal.

"I know that all the parents here tonight will understand it when I say having a child snatched from your life is like having an arm suddenly missing. There's never a sense of wholeness, never a moment of peace. To help me through the ordeal, I needed psychiatric treatment. But even that treatment wouldn't have seen me through if it hadn't been for the love and support of my family and friends, and especially my husband, Daniel, who never doubted that someday we would have our Suzy back."

Patty was flooded by a feeling of warmth from her audience. She began to relax again, knowing she had something important to say. "The message I want to send to all parents of missing children is never give up hope." She paused. "But I want to urge the rest of you—all those who will never know the personal agony of having a missing child—to do everything possible to help us keep pictures of our missing children in the eyes of the public."

She glanced down at her notes, not to read them but to center herself. When she began again, her voice was firm. "Statistics from the National Center for Missing and Exploited Children indicate that more than nineteen thousand children were reported missing last year. Unfortunately, that figure—as huge as it is—does not reflect the total number of missing children because there is no federal legislation requiring cases of kidnapped or missing children cases to be reported to the National Center."

She cleared her throat. "That's the first thing that we, as concerned parents and citizens, can do. We must support legislation requiring all such cases to be reported to a central agency."

As she spoke Patty noticed a child in the back of the room—a little girl with fluffy blond hair and bangs cut just the way she used to cut Suzy's. She faltered, then went on.

"It is imperative that pictures of all missing children be widely distributed. This is vitally important. We might never have gotten our Suzy back if someone hadn't seen her picture and notified the police."

She tried not to stare at the little girl in the back of the room. "Even if a child has been missing for a long time, modern computer science can use existing pictures to provide illustrations of how that child would look at his or her current age. The process is called age-progressed illustration. Pictures of our Suzanne were never age-progressed, and when we got her back, she had changed even more than I had expected.

"During the eleven months she was missing, I never stopped looking for her, trying to age-progress her in my mind. In every supermarket, in every parking lot, in every place where people gathered"—Patty felt her heart pounding. "Every place where people gathered, even in church, I found myself—I found myself . . ." Her voice wavered as she strained to get a better look at the little girl.

For a moment she felt disoriented, confused—as though she were waiting for something to happen. She was aware of a hushed stillness in the room, but her attention was focused on the child. A crazy, soaring hope engulfed her. She wanted to call to her, but her chest constricted and she couldn't breathe.

She became aware of polite coughs, of the stares of a sea of strangers. She opened her mouth, but no words came out and tears blurred her vision. She tried to go on, but her hammering pulse became a roar in her ears.

She was still looking. With a stab of pain, she realized what a part of her had always known. She could no longer deny it, and the realization made her weak.

Swaying, she sought Daniel's face in the front row, then clutched the sides of the lectern. She felt herself slipping, then Daniel's arms gripped her, and he led her gently from the podium.

"I'm sorry. I'm so sorry," she murmured as people crowded around them.

"Patty, this is my fault," Daniel said. "I should have known this would be too much for you."

People crowded near. "Can I help?" "Is she all right?"

"Home, Daniel. Please, take me home."

Someone drove them, and in the car Daniel held her close. She tried not to think, not to know what she knew, but oh, God, it was too late.

Patty heard the child crying as they entered the house. She pulled away from Daniel and ran to her.

"Shannon, Shannon, where's my Shannon? I don't know where she is." The child was sobbing, and Stella was trying to comfort her.

"Oh, Patty, I'm glad you're home. She fell right to sleep, but she woke up crying a little while ago."

"It's all right," Patty said, staring at the child. "I'll take care of her now."

Stella rose from her kneeling position at the side of the bed and quietly left the room.

Patty gathered the little girl in her arms. She knew Daniel was standing in the doorway, but she didn't look at him. Stroking the child, she rocked back and forth. "Mandy, Mandy, don't cry."

✹ 18 ✹

PHIL BENT A FEW PROCEDURES to get Shannon out on bail with record haste—managing, somehow, to keep the news of her release firmly under wraps.

He laid out everything he knew to Charlie Lawler and showed him the two letters he'd brought back from Los Angeles.

"Buchanan was set up, Charlie. I'm not sure by whom, but it's important that we don't tip our hand. Whoever it is will think he's in the clear as long as it looks like Buchanan is still a patsy."

Also, Phil patiently told his superior that with a little time and a little luck, he expected not only to clear Shannon but to locate the Marsh child—the real Suzanne Marsh—in the bargain.

"You're sure," Lawler asked, "that there's a tie between the snatch of the Marsh kid and the tip that led to Buchanan's arrest?"

"Absolutely. There's no question Mandy's death certificate was a plant," he pointed out. "Whoever planted it was resourceful enough to find a look-alike for the Marsh child in Mandy Knight, file false papers, and pose as a newspaper reporter to tip me off."

"And as long as Buchanan is charged with the snatch, his scam goes undetected." Lawler heaved his bulk from his chair and walked to face the window. "You realize, of course, we'll have egg on our face when all this eventually comes out. . . ." He returned to his chair. "Well, what the hell. I suppose we've had egg on our face before."

"Charlie," Phil reminded him, "we won't look so silly if I'm right about recovering the Marsh kid."

Lawler thought a minute. "The tip that led to Buchanan's being picked up—are you suggesting your man was behind that too?"

"Exactly," Phil said. "The tipster said he'd spotted Shannon in the Santa Barbara area. In fact, she was arrested up north—because of a flukey car breakdown that kept her here longer than the tipster had figured. Look, I've got a few leads—trust me on this—I think I can track him down. I need a few days and some travel expense."

Lawler nodded and jotted down a note. "Okay, Tewkes, you got it. But move fast. It won't be long before the press finds out Buchanan's out of jail."

With pitifully little in the way of possessions to collect, Shannon's release from jail was swift. Leaving her car impounded, only half listening to her joyful expressions of thanks, Phil hustled her into his Jeep and headed for the airport and the flight he had booked to San Diego.

He tried to talk to her on the plane, but she sat rigid beside him. It was her first flight, and though she longed to see her child, she had a hard time dealing with her fright.

"I have no idea how the Marshes are going to react," he told her. "If they really believe Mandy is their child, they'll fight me tooth and nail. Maybe they'll find the truth easier to accept when I tell them I'm convinced their daughter is alive and that I have a sketch of a man who may lead me to her."

As he spoke he opened his briefcase and withdrew Shannon's portrait of the man who had promised her a job. He studied it again. She'd drawn the man smiling, regular-featured, even handsome, except for a weak jawline.

"He smiled a lot," Shannon told him, "almost all the time. He admired my work, and he seemed so interested in me."

"No doubt," Phil said. "He was interested in where you came from and whether you could prove you were Mandy's mother."

Shannon was quiet for a moment. "Do you really think he had some connection with the woman who took Suzanne Marsh?"

"I'll bet you a new set of pastels that when we find your Mr. James Johnson, we won't be far from the kidnapper."

The flight attendant pushed a cart through the aisle, offering drinks.

"Could you use something, Shannon?" he asked her.

She nodded. "A Coke or maybe an orange juice. I'll pay for it—and yours too. You've done so much for me."

"They don't charge for orange juice, but if they did, it would be my treat. Tell you what, though," he said, smiling, "when that attorney in Texas liquidates your property, you can buy me a steak, how's that?"

She was quiet as she sipped her juice, but he saw her stiffen when the flaps were lowered and the engines cut power. She held tight to the armrests, and there was no mistaking her relief when the plane touched down. They had no baggage to collect, and he steered her to the car rental agency and signed for a small blue Ford.

Only after he'd negotiated the short freeway distance and saw Shannon's agitation grow did he tell her what he had in mind.

"I know how anxious you are to see Mandy, but you're going to have to trust me on this. I can't have you with me when I ring the Marshes' doorbell. I don't want to create a scene."

"But you have to tell them I'm her mother—"

"Shannon, of course I will. That's why we're here, to take Mandy back with us. I'm only asking you to wait in the car until the Marshes have had a chance to accept it." He reached over and took her hand, surprised at his own gesture.

She returned his grasp and, for a moment, seemed almost unwilling to let go. "Phil, I'll do whatever you tell me to do."

Her hand felt soft and small in his.

They drove past the Marsh house. It was small and square, like every other one on the block. But Phil noticed the tidy lawn, the neatly trimmed hedges, and the small bed of pansies and petunias that added a splash of color.

He parked a full block away. He steeled himself, weighing Shannon's eagerness to see her child against the pain he knew the Marshes would feel. He couldn't remember a time in his life when he'd had to do something so difficult. But looking at her, he found the courage he needed and got out of the car.

Phil expected Patty Marsh to be surprised to see him standing on her doorstep. But she gazed at him, utterly calm, making him even more uncomfortable.

"Mrs. Marsh." He tried for a way to begin.

"Are you here to get Mandy?" Her voice was flat.

"What?" he asked, not trusting what he'd heard.

"I asked if you were here to get Mandy." She sighed deeply, stepping aside to let him in. "You are. Of course you are."

Stunned, Phil followed her inside.

She led him into a sunny living room. "I didn't know Daniel had called you yet. He wanted to tell our families first."

Mystified, Phil sat on the couch. "He wanted to tell them what?"

She stared at him. "That . . . Mandy is not our child. If she is Mandy—I don't know, there's the death certificate. . . . Oh, God." Her eyes filled with tears.

Phil spoke gently. "Mrs. Marsh, the child is Amanda Knight. The death certificate is a fraud." He waited a moment for her to collect herself, then he started to ask, "When did you realize . . ."

"That she isn't Suzy?" She began to tell him something about giving a speech last night, about realizing she was still searching for her daughter, when something struck Phil. She had said her husband was planning to call up north. Once that call was made, the case would break wide open, and publicity was the last thing he wanted.

"Mrs. Marsh," he said, interrupting her. "Where is your husband now?"

"He left a little while ago—to see his mother."

Phil stood up. "Can you get him on the phone? I need to talk to him."

"Yes, I can try, but—"

"Please, Mrs. Marsh. It's important."

She went to the phone and dialed a number, said something Phil could not hear, then turned to hand him the receiver.

Phil was relieved when Marsh told him he had not yet told anyone—not even his mother—that Mandy was not their child. "I'm going to ask you to come home now, Mr. Marsh. There's something important you need to know."

As they waited for Daniel Marsh, Phil listened to Patty's story, but he heard children's voices coming from another part of the house. Mandy and the little Marsh boy.

Patty Marsh followed his glance. "Would you like me to get Mandy for you? I'll pack the clothes and toys we bought for her." For the first time, her voice quivered. "I know how her mother must feel—how anxious she must be to get her back."

Phil was relieved for the opening. "Mrs. Marsh, her mother is waiting outside in the car."

Patty stood up. "Go get her."

Phil admired her show of courage. "Mrs. Marsh, are you sure . . . ?"

"Go get her," she repeated. "I'll be all right."

When Shannon saw Phil coming, she jumped out of the car. "Did you see Mandy? Did you tell them?"

"Come on, Shannon," he said, his voice deliberately brusque to hide his feelings.

He led her to the house. Patty Marsh stood in the doorway holding Danny Joe by the hand. She turned, pointing down the hall. Neither she nor Shannon spoke.

Phil followed Shannon, realizing she was drenched in perspiration from sitting in the hot car. She was tense but smiling, like a child approaching a Christmas tree. The door to the children's room was open, and Phil watched Shannon's face light up at the sight of her daughter.

"Mandy," she said, softly. "Mandy."

Mandy looked up from her toys. Phil expected her to run to her mother, but she didn't. She looked startled, then thrust out her jaw. "*Where* were you, Shannon? I was waiting for you and waiting."

Rushing to her, Shannon picked her up. For a moment it seemed as if Mandy might pull away. Then the child burst out crying and buried her face against her mother's shoulder.

Phil turned quietly and left them alone.

Daniel Marsh had arrived and was standing in the living room, holding both his wife's hands. "Tewkes," he began, his voice husky, "you said you had something to tell us."

Marsh seemed anxious, but what Phil had to tell them couldn't be blurted out. "Sit down, please," he said. "It's a complicated story."

"Danny Joe," Patty said, heading him toward the kitchen, "get yourself a cookie and some milk."

Phil sat across from them, wondering how to begin, wondering how much he could safely tell them. He needed their cooperation, but he didn't want to hurt them any more than they'd been hurt already. "I know how difficult this has been for you," he began. "And how painful to realize Mandy is not your child."

He watched a range of emotions play across Daniel Marsh's face. "Undoubtedly by now," Phil went on, "you've read about a death certificate that was filed for Mandy Knight. I want to explain—"

"That's the one thing I can't understand," Marsh said, agitated. "She's not our daughter, but how can she be Amanda Knight if—"

"I've already explained to your wife that the death certificate was a plant."

"A plant," Marsh repeated. "What exactly do you mean by that?"

"Someone," Phil said, choosing his words carefully, "wanted to close the books on the kidnap of Suzanne Marsh—and almost succeeded by finding a look-alike in Mandy Knight and accusing her mother of being the kidnapper."

Patty Marsh leaned forward. "I want to be sure I understand you. Someone filed a false death certificate on Mandy? Why? Why would someone do that?"

"To make it appear that Mandy's mother—possibly in a state of grief over the supposed loss of her child—stole Suzanne."

"Are you saying," Daniel Marsh demanded, "that whoever did that was the real kidnapper?"

Phil shook his head. "Not exactly. The kidnapper, as you know, was a woman. I have reason to believe, based on information supplied by Mandy's mother, that the person who filed that death certificate was a man. But I'm convinced that when we find him, we will be that much closer to finding your daughter."

Tears welled in Patty Marsh's eyes. "Are you saying Suzy is alive? Oh, God, that is what you're saying, isn't it? You believe our Suzy is still alive."

Phil nodded, praying he was right—that he would not add to their suffering by disappointing them. "I think so, Mrs. Marsh," he said slowly. "But I need your cooperation—yours and your husband's—in order to see if I'm right."

Daniel Marsh rose abruptly and began to pace the small room. "What is it, precisely, that you want us to do?" His voice was full of uncertainty.

Phil took a breath. "The man we're looking for mustn't realize that his ruse has been discovered. I want you to go on pretending that the child you've brought home is Suzy."

Marsh looked as if Phil had lost his mind. "How on earth can we do that? Once you take her back to the Bay Area with you—"

"Then everyone will know," Patty Marsh finished his sentence, standing up abruptly. She looked directly at Phil. "Then Mandy must stay here with us. If it will help us get Suzy back, her mother must let Mandy stay here."

Phil did not realize Shannon was in the room until she spoke.

"Oh, no, Mrs. Marsh. I can't. I can't leave Mandy here. She has to go with me." She was carrying Mandy and her grip on the child tightened visibly.

Phil stood. "Wait a minute," he said. "Let's think this thing through together."

"There's nothing to think about," Patty Marsh said. "Mandy must stay with us, and if her mother won't leave without her, then her mother must stay here too."

She looked at Shannon. "You will stay, won't you? You will help us try to get our daughter back?"

Phil marveled at Patty's control and at how quickly she'd grasped the situation. He, too, looked at Shannon, waiting. He could not make the decision for her.

Mandy locked her legs around her mother's waist and buried her face in the curve of Shannon's neck.

Shannon stepped backward, as if she wanted to run. She looked from Patty to Daniel and finally to Phil. She met his gaze. "Is that what you want, Phil? Do you want me and Mandy to stay here?"

"If the Marshes will let you stay, I think it will solve a lot of problems. It won't be for long—just until I find our man."

"And Suzy," Patty broke in. "You're going to find Suzy."

Phil steadied himself. "I'll do my best, Mrs. Marsh. I can promise you that."

Mandy peeked out from her mother's shoulder. "Are we going to stay here with Mommy and Daddy, Shannon?"

Phil couldn't tell whether Shannon was laughing or crying. "Oh, Mandy. Oh, my baby."

✷ 19 ✷

PHIL FLEW HOME on Friday night, but spent most of the weekend at the station studying all the mug shots he could find. He was looking for someone who bore a resemblance to Shannon's portrait of Johnson, but he returned home Sunday night disgusted and very tired.

Moe squawked his customary rebuke as Phil entered the house, but Phil was grateful even for that welcome. He fed the bird, cleaned the scattering of sunflower-seed hulls from around the cage, and put his arm inside, inviting Moe to perch. But the bird attended to the business of eating. His attentions to Phil were over.

Phil had eaten a hamburger and fries at his desk, tasteless but enough to fill him. He wasn't hungry, but he peered into the refrigerator, knowing there was nothing he wanted, not even a beer.

When he'd left home on Friday, he'd half expected to have Shannon and Mandy with him when he returned, for lack of anywhere else to put them. He admired the Marshes, Patty especially, for agreeing to let Shannon and Mandy stay there. Without question, it was the best arrangement. Still, he admitted now, he felt a measure of disappointment. The empty house seemed cold.

It was too early to go to bed, too late to start work on his model even if he'd been in the mood. But there was always television, and it was almost time for Theresa's newscast.

Theresa was smiling, bright, confident. "Good evening, everyone. This is Terry Ames, bringing you an update on all the day's events."

He got comfortable in his chair but found himself curiously detached from the latest strife in Central America, plans for a new shuttle launch—even from a report of an unidentified woman whose body had washed ashore near Carmel. He felt sleepy. In a minute, he thought, he would switch off the set and head for bed.

"And this evening," Theresa said, as the picture dissolved to show a number of smiling, well-dressed people seated at dinner tables, "Monterey County District Attorney Roger Connelly and his wife, Lorelei, were warmly greeted at a five-hundred-dollar-a-plate dinner organized by Connelly to raise funds for college scholarships for the children of migrant workers and other young people who need extra incentives . . ."

Put off by the expensive show of political doings in the name of charity, Phil moved toward the set to turn it off. But he caught a flash of a handsome, blond head that arrested his attention. He stared, hoping to see the man again, but the segment was over.

Phil hesitated, thinking his mind was playing tricks on him, but he wanted another look at Shannon's sketch.

Getting it out of his briefcase, he studied the sketch done in three-quarter profile, the same view he'd seen of the man on the screen. The resemblance was real. The sketch looked like the man he'd glimpsed.

He stretched, rubbing the back of his neck. "Why would anyone involved in a kidnapping show himself in public at a political soiree?" he asked himself. He was tired, imagining things.

Closing his eyes, he tried to recapture the image of the man on television. He couldn't do it. Maybe, just to be sure, he should see that film clip again.

He called the television station and left a message for Theresa —Terry, he remembered to call her. "My name is Phil Tewkes.

She knows—used to know me. Tell her it's very important." He
left his number, hung up, and wondered if this whole thing was
just an excuse to call Theresa. "Well, hell," he muttered. "If it is
—why not? Probably long overdue."

Throwing a cover over Moe's cage, he went to bed. He didn't
know how long he'd been sleeping when the phone rang.

Fumbling, he picked it up. "Phil!" Theresa's voice was unmistakable. "I got your message. How are you?"

"I . . . hello, Theresa . . . Terry. I'm fine." He swung his legs
over the side of the bed. He forgot the sketch for a moment and
the man he'd seen. "It's really good to hear your voice."

She laughed. "Do you mean you don't hear me on the news?
I'm disappointed."

He started to tell her he watched her all the time, but he checked
himself, afraid his feelings would show. "As a matter of fact," he
began, "I saw your show tonight. That's why I called. It's a police
matter, nothing we're ready to go public with, but I sure could use
your help."

"Sounds intriguing," Terry said. "What can I do for you?"

"I need to see a replay of a film clip you showed tonight. Could
you arrange it? For sometime tomorrow?"

"Tonight's news?" she questioned. "No problem. I usually get
to the station about noon. Do you want to meet me there? I'll leave
a pass for you at the gate. I'm in building four."

"Sounds good. I'm looking forward to it." He was chagrined to
realize how much.

"Phil!" Theresa had her own office at the studio and was seated
behind a streamlined teak desk when Phil arrived. He'd never seen
her wearing glasses before, but she looked more vibrant, more
appealing than ever. She jumped up to greet him, throwing her
arms wide.

He stood awkward for a moment, then moved to embrace her.
"Terry . . . Theresa, it really is good to see you." Her touch, the
fragrance of her perfume made her real. She was Theresa again,

not just a smiling face on television. He surprised himself by kissing her, and she didn't seem to mind.

"Phil. It's great to see you. You look the same, too, even if your hair has lost some of its fire."

He smiled. "I hope it's just the hair."

Laughing, she moved back around her desk and picked up the phone. "Sit down. I'll call over and have the control room get that film clip set up. Did you want to see the whole thing?"

"No, just the part about the Connelly fund-raising dinner."

She put her hand over the receiver and looked at him. "The Connelly fund-raiser? Why would the sheriff have any interest in that?"

Phil laid a finger across his lips. "Let's call it a personal favor."

She looked at him—coquettishly, he thought—all the time she was talking on the phone. Phil would have liked to believe she meant something by it, but he suspected the only thing that was aroused was her reporter's instinct.

A young man holding out a sheaf of papers stuck his head in the doorway. "New copy for you, Terry," he said. "A bank holdup in Sausalito, film on its way, and they've identified that stiff who washed up on the beach last night. It's murder, according to the coroner. The woman's skull had apparently been bashed before she hit the water."

"Thanks," Terry said, coming around her desk to take the copy. "Tim, this is Investigator Phil Tewkes from the sheriff's office in Monterey. An old friend of mine." She turned back to Phil. "Though I hate to admit it, I am not wholly responsible for that articulate TV image. Tim is one of our staff writers. He gets half the credit."

Phil rose to shake the young man's hand, then followed Terry down the hall to a studio.

"I'll run the clip myself, John," she called toward the booth and, seating Phil at a small table, she began to run the tape fast forward.

"There!" Phil told her. "Can you freeze it there?"

Theresa stopped the tape. Phil studied the smiling, blond head he had seen the night before.

"What is it you're looking for, Phil? Or is that supposed to be a secret?"

Phil had not planned to tell her any more than was necessary, but now he was eager for a second opinion. "Theresa, I want you to look at a sketch," he said, taking it from his briefcase.

Theresa looked from the sketch to the screen. "Is there supposed to be a connection?"

"Well, I'm not entirely sure. That's why I want your opinion."

Theresa studied the sketch again. "It could be Neely Smith. See, there he is to the left on the screen, the blond man next to Connelly's wife."

She saw the resemblance. He hadn't imagined it. And it was somebody she knew. He tried to hide the excitement in his voice. "Who is Neely Smith?"

"He's relatively new up here, but he's Connelly's campaign manager. He has a law office in Monterey."

Phil was sitting in a hard-backed chair, but he leaned back and closed his eyes. The excitement he'd felt turned to disappointment. Smith was a prominent attorney. Hard to think someone in that position could be tied to a kidnapping.

"Phil, just what is this all about?"

He decided to level with her. "Theresa, this is a long shot, and it is definitely off the record. The man in that sketch is involved in a kidnapping and one hell of a clever cover-up. I have to know one way or the other whether he's the man on the screen."

Theresa stared at him. "You're serious. I know you. But Smith? Good God, Phil, he's one of Roger Connelly's oldest friends."

The picture was still frozen on the screen. They looked at it in silence. Then Theresa picked up the sketch. "Who drew this?" she asked.

Phil grimaced. "A woman who trusted the bastard a hell of a lot more than she should have."

Theresa was silent for a long moment, but he could see her

mind working. "Phil," she said quietly, "the Buchanan woman involved in the Marsh case is an artist. Did she do this drawing? Could this possibly have anything to do with that kidnapping?"

He was disquieted by her quickness of mind, by how easily she had made the connection.

His silence was apparently answer enough. "But I thought that case was closed. The Marshes have their daughter back, and Buchanan is going to trial. Surely you're not saying that Smith was involved with her? That's preposterous!"

She'd already realized more than he wanted her to know. Phil backed off. "Theresa, remember this is all off the record. When we're ready with a statement, you'll be the first—"

"Come on, Phil. You don't honestly believe that Neely Smith was involved in a kidnap scheme with Buchanan. It's something else, and I want to hear it. You owe me that much for old times' sake." She stood close, and he smelled again the spicy scent of her perfume.

He resisted the urge to kiss her. "I don't owe you anything, Theresa. The way I remember it, you owed me—and you just paid up with that film clip."

She stationed herself between him and the door. "I can help you if you let me. And I promise everything you tell me will be off the record until you give me a go."

He started to shake his head, but she persisted. "Really, Phil, I could help. Through the station I can get a fast rundown on Smith, more than you can get out of your police files. . . ."

Phil knew she was right. Smith was a prominent citizen, and he couldn't expect much on him from the police computer. "Okay, Theresa. You've got a deal. But I'm trusting you. There's an awful lot at stake if the story breaks."

"Let's go back to my office. I'll order us some sandwiches and coffee and get cracking on that rundown on Smith."

It surprised Phil to learn that a good photograph of Smith and a vitae were on file in the studio newsroom.

Theresa laughed at him. "There's nobody who is anybody in

the area that we don't have copy on. Never know when we're going to need it in a hurry," she said, handing him the vitae.

Phil scanned the report. Smith had grown up in a poor, multi-ethnic East Los Angeles neighborhood, graduated at the top of his class from Roosevelt High School, and gone on to Princeton on a scholarship. Graduated cum laude, stayed in the East until a little more than a year ago. He'd been in Los Angeles for a couple of months before setting up his office in Monterey and becoming Connelly's right-hand man. From there his vitae listed the usual claptrap, good works, et cetera, et cetera.

Theresa read over Phil's shoulder. "Not much to go on, is there?"

"It depends," he said. "To tell you the truth, at this point I don't know what I'm looking for. But I want the photo if that's okay."

"Be my guest. There's more where that came from."

An hour later Phil was at the post office. He mailed the photo of Neely Smith via overnight express to Shannon in San Diego.

✼ 20 ✼

ON SHANNON'S FIRST MORNING in the Marsh house, she'd jerked awake abruptly, uncertain of where she was. For a moment she thought she was still in jail, but then she saw the canopied youth bed where Mandy was sleeping. Getting up from a rollaway bed, she stared at Mandy, studying every feature on her face. The two weeks they'd been separated had been sheer hell, and Shannon knew how the Marshes must feel after being separated from their daughter for nearly a year.

Shannon glanced around. The room was painted a cheerful yellow, and yellow gingham checked curtains hung in the window. Stuffed animals and other toys lined one wall, and a butterfly mobile swayed gently from a hook above a chifforobe. For a little while Patty and Daniel had thought they had their Suzy back, and the room had been readied with joy and caring—but now they knew the child asleep in the bed wasn't their own.

Shannon blinked back tears. Phil Tewkes had come through for her when she'd needed him. If anyone could find their Suzy, he'd do it.

She felt awkward in the Marsh home, though she knew Patty and Daniel were trying hard to make her feel welcome. At first she tried to keep Mandy to herself, thinking it must hurt Patty to see the child, but Patty insisted they be part of the family.

"You don't have to stay in the bedroom all the time," Patty told her that first day. "And . . . Mandy likes to play with Danny Joe and feed the cat."

The feeling of love that permeated the Marsh household was a revelation to Shannon. There was no mistaking Patty's nervousness. Every time the phone rang she jumped up, hoping, Shannon was certain, that it would be Phil with news of Suzy. But despite her anxiety, Patty was affectionate to Danny Joe and to Mandy too. Daniel was a caring father, a devoted husband.

It was vastly different from Shannon's own childhood home, a waxed and polished mausoleum where she'd been made to feel like an interloper, skulking around the heavy furniture, hardly more noticed than if she'd been invisible.

Here, Danny Joe and Mandy ran noisily through the small rooms, letting screen doors bang satisfactorily behind them as they clattered out to the backyard. They returned with scraped knees, wilted daisies, and an enthusiasm that was always shrill.

They had all agreed that Mandy should continue to call Patty "Mommy" and Daniel "Daddy," just in case a friend or relative arrived for an unexpected visit. Secrecy was important. Word must not get out—and possibly back to the kidnapper—that the Marsh case had been reopened. But Shannon felt strange every time she heard Mandy address Patty as Mommy.

"It's cute to hear Mandy calling someone Mommy," she told Patty, trying to convince herself it was true. "She's never called me anything but Shannon."

Despite the Marshes' kindness, Shannon was eager to leave. She understood why Phil wanted her to stay, however, and she would stay as long as he told her to. Meantime, she'd try to make herself useful by doing small chores.

Patty seemed busy all the time, but there was a distracted air about her, as if she wasn't really paying attention to what she was doing. Unobtrusively, Shannon found ways to help her.

On Monday evening Shannon already felt familiar enough in the kitchen to set the table for dinner. As she worked she glanced out the window to the backyard, where Danny Joe and Mandy were sending stuffed animals down a makeshift slide, squealing with laughter and racing to catch the toys as they fell. Shannon bit her lip as she realized how much Mandy had missed by having so little contact with other children.

But they had money now, she and Mandy, thanks to Miss Ida. When this whole mess was behind them, she'd find them a nice place to live—a place where Mandy could have friends and play in a nice yard. From now on her daughter would have a better home than the back seat of a car.

When Patty walked into the kitchen, Shannon asked, "Would you like me to make a salad?"

Patty took hamburger patties out of the refrigerator. She started to unwrap them, then suddenly she jerked around and looked at Shannon, as if first realizing Shannon had spoken.

"What did you . . . oh, a salad . . . yes, of course. That would be very nice."

"If you have cabbage, I can make very good cole slaw. My grandmother taught me, and I used to make it for the woman I lived with in Texas."

Patty wiped her hands on a towel, then rummaged in a refrigerator drawer. "I don't think so. Wait—here's a cabbage. I guess I'd forgotten I bought it."

Shannon found a bowl and a sharp knife and began shredding the cabbage into neat, thin shreds, the way she'd been taught by the grandmother who'd shown her the only love and affection she'd known as a child. Grandma had been dead for years, but Shannon could never make the slaw without thinking of her.

She was trying to mix exactly the right proportions of mayonnaise and vinegar when the screen door slammed. "Mommy, Mommy," Danny Joe shouted, holding out an old, tattered bear. "Gordy got a boo-boo. He fell off the slide. You have to kiss it and make it well."

Mandy, her tiny face smudged with grime, watched big-eyed as Patty Marsh kissed the bear on the tummy, then inspected it from top to bottom. "Well, look here," Patty said, more attentive now. "No wonder Gordy hurts. He's got a torn seam on his side. I'll fix him right after supper."

Danny Joe led Mandy down the hall to wash up. "See, I told you Mommy could make him well."

Shannon smiled, but she felt as if a heavy weight was pushing against her chest. She hoped that when she took Mandy away, she could make such a caring home for her.

Daniel came in from the backyard. "If those burgers are ready, I've got the barbecue fired up."

They ate on a little patio just outside the kitchen door. Daniel had three helpings of the cole slaw, and Patty asked for the recipe.

"It's even better after it sets for a while," Shannon told them shyly.

They sat outside until dusk, then Daniel offered to get both children ready for bed while Patty and Shannon did the dishes.

"He'll tell them a bedtime story," Patty told Shannon. "But before we get started on the dishes, I'd better fix that bear."

Shannon followed Patty into the living room, but when Patty turned on the television and picked up a wicker sewing basket, Shannon returned to the kitchen. If she hurried, she might have the dishes all done and the kitchen tidied before Patty came to help.

Suddenly, Patty's scream tore through the house.

When Shannon rushed back to the living room, Patty was kneeling in front of the television set. A picture of a woman filled the screen, and a newscaster's voice was saying, " . . . but police in Monterey County have now established that the dead woman is Helen Hanson, who was reported missing from her Los Angeles home several weeks ago."

"It's her," Patty gasped. "That's the woman who stole Suzanne."

It was late evening when Phil arrived home from his meeting with Theresa. He heard his phone ringing as he put the key in the lock, but it stopped before he could answer it. He went into the bedroom to change his clothes, and it started to ring again.

"Tewkes," he said, the receiver tucked under his chin as he shrugged out of his shirt.

"Phil! Thank God, you're finally home."

"Shannon, what is it? What's happened?"

He heard her take a deep breath. "Mrs. Marsh thinks she saw her on television—the woman who kidnapped Suzanne. They say her body washed ashore near Carmel—"

Phil remembered the report.

"Mrs. Marsh wants to call the local police, but I begged her to wait until she talked to you. On TV they showed a photograph of the woman the way she looked before she died. Mrs. Marsh thinks it's her—"

"Put Mrs. Marsh on the phone."

Patty Marsh's voice was tense. "They showed her picture for only a few seconds, Investigator Tewkes, but I'm sure she's the woman who stole my baby. They said her name was Helen Hanson."

"How sure are you, Mrs. Marsh? Can you identify a woman you saw only once—a year ago—on the strength of a photo flashed on the screen?"

The voice wavered. "I could be positive if I could hear her voice. She had such an odd way of speaking."

Phil sat on the bed. "You mentioned that before—a nasal quality. You said you thought she had a cold."

"Yes, except I don't think it really was a cold. I don't know. It just sounded strange. Now, if she's dead, I'll never be able . . ." Patty's voice trailed off.

The odds that the dead woman was Suzanne's abductor seemed incredibly slim. But were they slimmer, he wondered, than his thinking the man he'd seen on television might be the man in Shannon's sketch?

He listened patiently as Patty Marsh repeated everything she could remember about Suzanne's abductor, but his mind leapt ahead to conjectures he was almost afraid to make: *If she was right and the dead woman had taken Suzanne, was her murder connected to the kidnapping?*

He visualized the face of the man he'd seen on the screen, the man who so strongly resembled Shannon's sketch. Could there be a connection between Neely Smith and the murdered Helen Hanson?

Phil understood why the Marshes would want to go public, but maybe he could convince them that, for the moment, there was more reason to keep it quiet. Smith—if Smith was actually involved—probably knew where Suzanne Marsh was, and they didn't dare do anything that might jeopardize finding the child alive.

"Mrs. Marsh," he said evenly, "I know how anxious you are, but I may be onto something up here. Do you remember the sketch of a man I showed you Friday—the man you said you'd never seen before? There's a chance—just a chance—that I've discovered who he is. I think he may be connected to the kidnapper. If I'm right—and if Helen Hanson was Suzanne's abductor—then we need to keep this under wraps until I have a chance to prove it."

Patty Marsh could hardly get the words out. "Do . . . do you think he . . . he might have Suzy?"

"I don't think he has her, Mrs. Marsh, but I think he may know where she is."

Fear crept into Patty Marsh's voice. "But you think he might have killed Helen Hanson. Isn't there a chance— Oh, God, my Suzy—what has he done with Suzy. . . ?"

"I don't know yet, Mrs. Marsh," Phil said gently, "that's exactly why I'm asking you to keep this quiet."

She was silent, but Phil could almost hear her unspoken thoughts. He wished he could give her more reassurance.

"How much time do you think you'll need?"

"I wish I could answer that. But I promise you I'll try to keep you advised and that I'll move as quickly as I can."

He heard her sigh. "All right," she said finally. "Oh, God, if I could just hear that woman's voice. . . ."

Phil's mind had moved into high gear. "First, I want to see if

Shannon can make a positive ID of my suspect. If she can, then I'll see if I can turn up any connection between him and the murdered woman. Please, Mrs. Marsh, put Shannon back on the phone."

He explained to Shannon about the photo he'd mailed to her. "It'll arrive in the morning," he said. "Study it carefully. This man is well known up here, Shannon, and there's no room for a mistake. But if you recognize him as your 'James Johnson,' I'll want you to fly back here right away to make a positive ID."

✁ 21 ✁

It was eight in the morning when Phil tracked down Robb Simpson, the investigator assigned to the Hanson case. He was having breakfast in a downtown coffee shop, and Phil ambled over to his table. "Mind if I join you?"

By way of greeting, Simpson waved the piece of toast he was holding and continued chewing.

Phil sat down across from him and signaled the waitress to bring him coffee. "I hear you're working the Hanson case."

Simpson nodded. He was older than Phil, tall and lanky, laconic, but a thorough homicide investigator.

"What do you know about Hanson?" Phil asked.

Simpson shrugged. "Thirty-seven, never married." He gulped his coffee. "Her mother reported her missing twelve days ago. Probably bought it right after she disappeared, because the coroner says she was in the drink ten to twelve days."

Phil noted the information. "Any rap sheet on her?"

"Clean as fresh rain," Simpson said, spreading jam on another slice of toast. "Went to work, went home, few friends. Reported to have been under stress before she disappeared."

"Nobody knew why?"

"Not that we've found. Apparently, she didn't get close to anyone."

"What about a boyfriend or a busted romance?"

Simpson shook his head. "From what we've heard, she shied away from men. Had a speech defect from a cleft palate. Made her self-conscious."

Phil's senses quickened. *A cleft palate.*

Simpson put down his fork, mounded with hash browns. "Why the interest, Tewkes?"

Phil sipped his coffee. "She may tie into a case I'm working on—but it's something I have to keep under wraps until I have more to go on."

Simpson half smiled. "Help you all I can—but it's got to be reciprocal, buddy."

"Absolutely," Phil said, flipping open his notebook, "as soon as I'm sure of the connection. You said she was thirty-seven, unmarried. What kind of work did she do?"

Simpson shoveled in another mouthful of potatoes. "She was the head clerk at a hospital in L.A. County."

Phil stopped writing in the middle of a word. "What hospital?"

"U.S.C. Medical Center—you know it, don't you—the county hospital right off the San Bernadino freeway near downtown?"

Phil nodded. *Bingo.* "I know it," he said, his voice soft.

Simpson gave him another half smile. "Fitting into your game plan?"

Phil nodded. "You better believe it," he said.

Simpson got up from the table, picked up both checks, and threw down some change. "Your coffee's on me. I got work to do—but you know where to find me when you have anything."

Phil watched Simpson leave, glad to be alone. He was barely able to contain his excitement, but instead of following his first impulse and bolting out of there and heading for the station, he accepted a refill on his coffee. Sipping it, he ticked off what he knew.

Helen Hanson was from Los Angeles and had been a head clerk at County-U.S.C. Medical Center. She certainly would have known how death certificates were filed. And she had a speech defect. A defect that might have sounded to Patty Marsh like someone with a bad cold.

Phil stared at his notebook, no longer writing. If Shannon could make a positive ID of Smith, and if he could establish a link between Smith and Hanson . . .

He took a final slug of coffee and left, anxious to make a phone call.

He found what he needed in the yellow pages, dialed a number, and reached an answering service.

"Dr. Ford's exchange."

"This is Investigator Phil Tewkes at the sheriff's office in Monterey. I need to reach the doctor for some important information," he said. "Can you put me through right away?"

The woman hesitated. "I'll try, sir," she said. "I'm going to put you on hold." A moment later the voice was back. "All right, sir, Doctor is on the line. I can connect you now."

"Dr. Ford. Phil Tewkes at the sheriff's station. We need information from a specialist, but it should take only a minute."

"Yes." The doctor's voice was crisp. "What can I do for you?"

"If you can, Dr. Ford, would you tell me what kind of a speech defect a person with a cleft palate would have?"

"A cleft palate?" the doctor echoed. "There usually wouldn't be any speech defect—not if corrective surgery was done early enough and correctly."

Phil frowned. "Well, suppose surgery wasn't done early enough —or correctly. If there *was* a speech defect, what would it be like?"

The doctor sounded curt. "When the patient talked, air would escape through the nose. The voice would have a nasal quality."

A nasal quality. "As though the speaker had a cold?"

"Well, actually it's the opposite of a cold. That is, the passages are opened rather than closed. But I suppose to a lay person it might sound like a cold."

"Thanks, Dr. Ford. You've been a big help."

It was barely nine-thirty, probably too early for the photo to
have arrived in San Diego. He headed for the station, but the
moment he arrived he slammed into his office and dialed the
Marshes' number.

"Oh, Phil!" Shannon was breathless. "It just arrived a little
while ago. It's him, Phil, I'm sure of it. That is James Johnson.
Even Mandy recognized him."

Phil nodded, caught between exhilaration and fear. What a can
of worms . . . *the DA's campaign manager.*

"Shannon, tell the Marshes not to talk to anyone about this.
And you get on a plane and get back up here. I want you to—"

"Wait, Phil," Shannon interrupted. "What about Mandy? I'm
not leaving here without her."

"Shannon, for the time being, she'd be better off—" He
stopped in mid-sentence, realizing Shannon meant what she'd
said. There was no point in arguing with her. "Okay, bring
Mandy. When you book the flight, call me here at the office and
give me the flight number. If I'm not here, leave a message. Say
you're Mrs.—" He stopped, trying to think of a name. "Oh, hell,"
he said, "you won't have any trouble thinking of a name. I'll know
it's you."

He had one last thing to do before he went in to see Lawler,
and it didn't take very long. A young clerk in the records room
brought Phil a copy of Simpson's preliminary report on the Hanson
case, and he studied the intricate set of details that had led to the
identification of the corpse. There was nothing significant in the
report that he didn't already know, but he wasn't taking any chances
on missing a useful detail. This was his case now, *his.* Professional
and personal.

Lawler had several people in his office, and Phil waited nearly
an hour to get him alone. Finally, he stormed in. "I've got to talk
to you, Charlie. It won't hold."

Lawler cleared the room, then turned to Phil. "So what's up?"

Phil didn't waste time on preliminaries. "Helen Hanson—the

body that washed ashore near Carmel—is the woman who snatched the Marsh child. Patty Marsh is ready to make a positive ID, and I have good supporting evidence."

Charlie Lawler whistled. "All right. Not bad. So what's your evidence?"

Phil shook his head. "I'll get to that. First, there's something else—and you'd better hold on to your hat for this one." He paused. "I think I know who her accomplice was—the man who engineered the Marsh kidnapping—the man who called himself James Johnson."

The big man nodded appreciatively, folded his hands behind his head, and leaned back in his chair. "So lay it all out."

Phil stared at him for a minute. "Charlie, I can't prove it yet, but I know the proof is out there. Helen Hanson's accomplice was Neely Smith—Roger Connelly's campaign manager."

Charlie Lawler leaned forward. "Phil, if you're serious, you need another vacation. Smith is the DA's right-hand man."

"I know that, Charlie," Phil insisted. "Listen to what I've got." He took Shannon's portrait of James Johnson out of a manila folder and laid it in front of Lawler. "Look like Smith to you, does it, Charlie?"

Lawler grunted, affirmative.

Point by point, Phil explained everything. "What I need now is to find the link between Smith and Hanson. I know it's out there."

Charlie Lawler looked doubtful. "I think you're pissing up the wrong tree." He leaned heavily across his desk, reminding Phil of a beached whale. "But if we're investigating a close associate of his, we'd better let the DA know about it."

"Charlie, maybe it would be better to wait until—"

Lawler slammed the desk with his fist. "No way. We're going to tell him now. Connelly's new and he may not be the DA for all that long, but I'm not going to have him find out what we're doing and come down on us like a raging bull."

Lawler picked up the phone. "Listen, Phil, this is a pal of his you're talking about. You may not know it, but the DA can be mean when he's mad."

Lawler spoke into the receiver. "The district attorney's office," he said. "And I want to talk to him personally. Tell him it's very important."

Fifteen minutes later, Phil and Charlie Lawler stood outside the door to Roger Connelly's office.

"After you," Lawler said, grimly.

As they entered Connelly walked around his desk to greet them. Smiling, he shook hands with Lawler and then with Phil. "It's good to see you, Phil," he said. "From the little bit that Charlie told me, it sounds as if you've got a big one by the tail."

Connelly motioned for them to sit down, and Phil eased himself into a huge, mahogany-colored leather chair. Lawler sat down, too, and Connelly leaned against the near side of his desk. Folding his arms, he looked at Phil. "What do you have to tell me?"

Composing himself, Phil glanced around the room. A sleek sideboard ran almost the length of one wall—the liquor cabinet, Phil surmised. Paintings—originals if he guessed right—adorned the walls. The whole place had class and distinction—like the man himself.

Connelly had a presence. Phil felt it now, and he'd felt it in the past. Roger Connelly was bright, articulate, and extremely sure of himself. His confidence was tempered by a genuine friendliness despite the fact that he was turning out to be a tough DA.

At first Phil had thought Connelly was just a playboy, a figurehead almost—appointed after the sudden death of the DA—who would simply be a caretaker in the office until the next election was held. But in the three months Connelly had held the office, Phil had learned to respect and like him. He felt comfortable with him, too, although now—with Lawler and Roger both staring at him—he felt as if he were back in school and an angry teacher had marched him down to see the principal. Phil's own confidence was shaken. Surely, a close friend of this man couldn't be a kidnapper—possibly a murderer.

"Phil," Roger Connelly repeated, looking attentive. "Let's have it. You two have my curiosity up."

Phil cleared his throat. "Before Shannon Buchanan was released on bail, I asked her—"

"Wait a minute," Connelly cut in smoothly. "I didn't know she was out on bail."

"Since last Friday," Phil told him. "She was able to raise bail."

"I see," Roger said. "I haven't been in the office since Thursday. I spent the weekend in San Francisco. So many people flew in to attend a charity dinner we arranged—"

Phil broke in. It was time to tell him—no more hedging. "I saw a film clip of your fund-raiser. And in the clip I saw a man I thought I recognized from this portrait." He took Shannon's drawing out and handed it to Connelly.

Connelly stared at it for a long time. "It looks something like Neely Smith." He handed the picture back to Phil. "But of course it isn't Neely—is it?"

"Roger, we don't know," Lawler broke in. "Buchanan drew that—but she could have seen Smith at any one of a dozen places and confused him with someone else."

"The Buchanan woman? How does she figure into this?" Roger Connelly's easy smile was gone. He was staring hard at Phil.

"Buchanan drew the sketch to identify someone we now think may have been involved in the Marsh kidnapping. It's not easy telling you this," Phil said, "but I think Neely Smith may be that man." Phil paused. "And that he may have been involved not only in the kidnapping but also in a murder."

There wasn't a sound in the room.

Phil cleared his throat, then began explaining his case to the district attorney. As he talked his confidence returned. He *knew* what he was talking about. He wasn't off on some half-assed tangent. And the look that settled on Connelly's face told Phil that the district attorney was taking what he had to say very seriously.

Suddenly, Roger kicked at a wastebasket and sent it flying across the room. Then he walked away and stood with his back to them, staring out the window. "My God. Not again. The whole thing is happening again."

Phil heard a catch in Roger's voice. "What do you mean? *What's* happening again?"

Roger hit the window frame with his fist, then turned back to face the two men. "Déjà vu. You see, I've been through this once before." He took a long, shuddering breath. "I didn't believe it then. I didn't want to believe it. Maybe—maybe I should have. . . ."

He walked back to his desk and sat down. He looked solemn, but his composure had returned. "Gentlemen," he began, his manner almost formal, "Neely Smith and I go back a long way. We attended college together. We were roommates, in fact. . . ."

He paused, and for Phil it seemed like a long wait before he continued. "There was a girl at Princeton—I don't even remember her name, but back then everyone knew her. She was a tramp— oh, well, that doesn't matter. The fact is," he said, putting a hand over his eyes, "the fact is . . . she was murdered."

Connelly rose and moved slowly to the window, striking an open palm with his fist. "Her body was found near the campus. She had been bludgeoned to death, and the last people known to have seen her alive reported she'd been with Neely Smith that afternoon."

Phil listened quietly.

Roger continued, but he did not face them. He turned his head sideways, talking over his shoulder in a voice heavy with emotion. "I was in our room the whole evening of the murder. . . . Neely admitted he'd seen the girl earlier, but he swore he had nothing to do with her death. I believed him, of course I believed him. Neely could never have done anything like that . . . bludgeon someone to death with a rock. . . ."

Roger sighed. "Anyway, the coroner fixed the time of death at something like seven or eight that evening. Neely said he'd been in our room all evening, and as far as I knew, that was true. There were other guys in the house who swore he'd been there. . . ."

Baffled, Phil asked, "If you were in the room with him, then obviously he wasn't the murderer. . . ."

"That's it," Roger groaned. "I *was* in the room, but I slept for an hour, maybe longer. I took Neely's word for it—I believed him—all these years. Could I have been wrong about him?"

Now Roger turned to look at them. "The girl's murder was never solved—I vouched for him . . . we vouched for him. Now, if he's involved in this, as you say . . . I don't know. I just don't know."

The district attorney sighed deeply, and for the first time Phil saw him bereft of his confidence and charisma. Phil felt sorry for him. He was a decent guy, and in one hell of a rotten position.

Lawler interrupted. "There was no proof then that Smith was involved in that murder. For all we know, we could be wrong on this one. We've got to follow it through, but, after all, the drawing you saw was made by a transient—we don't know how reliable she is."

Phil was surprised at the vehemence with which he'd been about to defend Shannon when the DA cut in.

"Her reliability is not the issue here," Roger said. "If Phil thinks he's got enough evidence to pursue an investigation of Smith, then of course he'll have to go ahead."

Phil was filled with admiration for this man who, even with rumors growing that he was going to run for governor, was willing to pursue an investigation of his personal friend and campaign manager.

"Roger," Phil said, trying to keep the sympathy out of his voice, "Buchanan drew the portrait to describe a man who called himself James Johnson. From what we've learned, this Johnson used Buchanan to close the books on the Marsh kidnapping—and he may have murdered Helen Hanson, whom we now believe committed the kidnapping and filed a false death certificate for Buchanan's child."

Phil thought he detected a glint of admiration in Roger's prolonged stare. "What I need to do now," he continued, "is to find the connection between Neely Smith and Helen Hanson. And of course," he added, "it's important for Buchanan to identify Smith in person as the man she knew as James Johnson."

Phil rose, aware of the toll this was taking on the district attorney. "Look, I'm sorry, but . . ."

Roger's smile was sad. "Phil, you're just doing your job—and you're doing it well, I might add. You're right. Buchanan will have to identify Neely. Where is she now?"

Phil looked at his watch. "She and her daughter should be on a plane on their way up from San Diego. I should check on the flight. I intend to meet them."

"Neely is in San Francisco. He'll be home tomorrow or Wednesday. I'd rather have him come home on his own and then call him into the office. Meantime, where is Buchanan going to stay?"

Phil stopped short, not wanting to say he'd planned to take her and Mandy to his house. "Maybe . . . maybe a motel, I guess," he said.

Roger shook his head. "I've got a better idea. We want her someplace where she'll be safe—and where the media can't get hold of her. And we don't want Neely to know we're investigating him or he might decide to run. As a matter of fact, in case you're thinking of it, I wouldn't put a tail on him. He'll panic—I know Neely— if he's actually involved and realizes he's under surveillance."

Roger paced the room. "Neely's always alert. He would notice a tail—I'm sure of it. And if he realized he was under suspicion, he might decide to bolt. We certainly don't want to risk that."

He stopped pacing and turned to Phil. "Listen," he said. "My family has a cabin in the mountains, about a forty-five-minute drive from here. Phil, if I gave you the keys and directions, you could take Buchanan and the child there. They're welcome to any food in the house, and the cupboard should be pretty well stocked."

Phil nodded. Maybe it wasn't a bad idea at that. He felt grateful to Roger. The district attorney was considerate and alert even now when he was under pressure. Maybe, he thought, putting the portrait in his briefcase, Roger would make a fine governor.

Phil reached for the phone. "If you don't mind, I'd better check and see when her plane is coming in." Calling the station, he asked if he had any messages.

"Yes," the desk officer told him. "A Mrs. Valentine said to tell you she and her daughter would arrive at 4:20 p.m." He told Phil the airline and flight number.

"Phil," Roger asked, "what's our next move?"

"First thing tomorrow I'm going down to L.A. and dig into Hanson's background—and Smith's. I'll need a search warrant and a letter to take to the LAPD. . . ."

"Phil, you can have all the backup you need."

Something in Phil bristled. He shook his head. "I can handle this one alone."

Roger gave him the key to the cabin, they shook hands, and Phil left, heading for the airport to pick up Mrs. Valentine.

❧ 22 ❧

NEELY SMITH REMAINED in San Francisco on Monday, supervising the final accounting of the charity dinner Sunday night and paying court to several celebrities who had attended. The event had been his idea and he had planned it himself, even to approving the dinner menu.

They had raised nearly forty-two thousand dollars, more than expected—but the money wasn't important. What was important was that the extensive publicity would show Roger as a concerned and involved citizen, worthy of serious consideration as a contender for governor.

Neely should have felt pleased with his success, but instead he was apprehensive. Something was bothering Roger, and Neely had a cringing feeling that the *something* involved him.

On Tuesday morning he phoned Roger from his hotel room in San Francisco. Roger sounded strange, distant, nothing like his usual cheerful style. Neely told him what they had netted and how much coverage they had received, expecting enthusiastic appreciation, but Roger hardly responded.

"You'll be home tonight?" Roger asked.

"Yes, do you want me to come by?"

"No," Roger said, sharply. "I just want to know where you're going to be. I'll phone you this evening."

Roger had hung up then, leaving Neely wondering.

After checking out of the hotel, Neely had headed to the airport for the short flight back to the Bay. He tried to reassure himself. Roger couldn't be onto anything—not onto *that* anyway. By the time he reached his condo, he had all but convinced himself that he had nothing to worry about.

Nothing to worry about.

He would have preferred a martini, but he mixed himself a short gin and tonic instead. These days he didn't dare operate without full control of his faculties. He went through his mail, then scanned the headlines of the newspaper. He flipped it open, and there she was—staring at him from the third page.

Helen Hanson.

The paper lay on the kitchen counter, and he slumped forward, catching the edge of the counter in his midsection as he read:

> . . . a body that washed ashore at Monterey Bay has been identified as Helen Hanson, who was reported missing from her Los Angeles home almost two weeks ago. Investigators say that Hanson, a hospital clerk, was a murder victim and that her skull was crushed before she was put in the water.
>
> Captain Eugene Burgess of the shore patrol speculated today that the body had been dumped from well out in the Bay. "If it had been dumped closer in, it would have come ashore much sooner," he said. "The condition of the body suggests it was put in the ocean close to the breakwater, possibly by someone who thought that from that point at sea, the tide would carry the body southward."
>
> According to Burgess, "if the body had caught the outgoing tide, it probably would not have come ashore for months, making identification nearly impossible. . . ."

Even as he read the article Helen's smiling face seemed to be staring at him. He could almost hear her strange, nasal voice repeating, "I love you, Neely. I love you."

When she first came to see him after he opened an office in Los Angeles, he hadn't remembered her face. But when she spoke her voice brought back memories of a thin, friendless girl whom he'd gotten to know during long study sessions in the public library.

Not many classmates from his poor East Los Angeles neighborhood had been devoted scholars, determined, as he was, to use education for passage to a better life. But night after night Helen had sat across from him in the library, and they'd become friends. He'd enjoyed having someone to tell about his big plans for the future, and she'd always been awed.

"You're really going to do it, Neely. You're going to be all the wonderful things you say you're going to be."

Back then her encouragement had been a needed boost to his ego, but when she tracked him down after he returned to California, he'd had no use for her.

"You did it, Neely," she murmured, staring at him wide-eyed. "I always knew you'd be a success . . . and maybe, sometime, I can be of help to you."

Neely stayed behind his big oak desk—one of the few things he'd salvaged when his law practice in New York had folded— maintaining a distance from Helen. His office, which he thought of as temporary, was on the third floor of a bank building, near Chinatown, that had seen better days.

"Maybe I can help you build your new practice," she said hesitantly. "I work at U.S.C. Medical Center. It's a very poor neighborhood. We get a lot of accident victims who need attorneys. Occasionally, when people die, their families need an attorney— sometimes girls give up their babies for adoption."

The idea that she thought she could help him galled Neely, but when he didn't respond, she continued, "I . . . I work with private attorneys to arrange placements."

"I'll keep you in mind," he'd said sarcastically. He had risen then, letting her know it was time for her to leave.

At the doorway she'd turned back, staring at him.

He'd forced a smile. "It was good to see you, uh, Helen, and don't worry, I'll keep you in mind if and when I need the help."

And then, only a few months later, he *had* needed her help. He'd needed to find an adoptable child. Still staring at Helen's picture in the newspaper, Neely gritted his teeth, remembering.

He had phoned her and told her the sort of child he hoped to find. "They don't want an infant, but I thought if you had contacts, you might still be able to help. They want a young child, one that's past the age where it cries all the time. The man would prefer a girl, and they both say it needs to be an attractive child. . . ."

It was a long shot. He never really expected to hear from her, but then he had. She called and described the perfect child. "The mother died," she told him, "and the father doesn't want to keep her. I can bring her to your office."

She'd been right. The child was perfect, just what he asked for. Maybe he should have been suspicious when she wouldn't accept a fee, but he hadn't been. He'd had no idea there was a problem until nearly ten months later—long after he'd been settled in Monterey—when she'd called him again, almost hysterical, early on a Sunday morning.

"Neely, it's me, Helen. I've got to talk to you." She'd been excited, and her speech, always difficult to understand, was garbled. "I have to see you right away."

Neely had been more annoyed than concerned. "I'm awfully busy just now, Helen," he'd said. "I'm sure you can understand—"

She'd interrupted him, her voice edging toward hysteria. "Her picture is all over! On milk cartons and posters—everywhere I look I see her."

"See who?" he'd asked, feeling increasingly annoyed.

"Suzanne Marsh. The little girl that I . . . I only did it for you . . ." Helen burst out sobbing, and then the premonition that something was terribly wrong snaked up Neely's spine.

"Helen, get hold of yourself," he'd said, "and tell me what this is all about."

"You'll hate me, Neely. You'll be very angry. I don't know what I was thinking of. I love you, Neely. I've always loved you, ever since we were in school. I wanted to do something—anything—to make you love me. I took her, Neely. I took the little girl, because you needed her, and I thought you'd stay in touch—but then you moved away and now her picture is all over. . . ."

Neely hadn't breathed. *My God, what was she saying?* His pulse began to race. "You took—kidnapped—the baby that you brought up here—that I . . ." He shook his head. "No," he'd said sharply. "You had papers. A consent form from the father, the mother was dead—"

"No, no," she'd wailed. "I got the release papers at the hospital. I filled them out myself. But, Neely, I only did it for you. Remember, I didn't want any money."

Neely had reeled, but he always came through in a crisis. "Helen," he'd commanded, "come up to the Bay tomorrow. When you get to the Monterey airport, phone me and I'll tell you where to meet me." He'd slammed down the phone then, wanting to be sick, but knowing he had to keep his head clear to think his way through this.

He'd decided to meet her on the *Lorelei II*, the Connelly boat. That way no one could see her entering his condo, and on the pier she'd be just another person in the crowd.

First of all, he told himself, he needed proof that he'd had no idea the child he'd placed for adoption had been kidnapped. Once he had that proof, he'd decide what to do next.

When Helen called from the airport, he told her how to get to the boat. He arrived before she did, and he set up his tape recorder below deck. He turned it on, saying a few words into it to make sure it was working. When he played it back he heard the water lapping against the side of the boat, the gulls crying overhead, and his own voice, tense and afraid.

The tape.

Turning suddenly, Neely knocked over his gin and tonic. Ignoring it, he hurried into the living room and lifted a painting of a skyline off the wall. The tape was there, carefully wrapped and tacked to the back of the picture. He jerked the tape off the picture and stared at it in his hand. Then, compulsively, he put the tape in the recorder and turned it on:

Helen, come on down. I'm in the galley.

Neely, Neely, I'm so sorry. Oh, Neely, I hope you can understand. I was just trying to help you, to show you that I care, because—

He'd interrupted. *Helen, sit down and listen carefully to the questions I'm going to ask you. This is very important.*

Yes, Neely, yes.

When you first contacted me, you told me you sometimes worked with attorneys for various things, including helping mothers place their babies for adoption. . . .

Yes, yes, I said that, but it wasn't true. I never helped arrange an adoption. I never did any of those things I told you I did. I . . . I made it all up, just hoping you'd stay in touch with me—hoping I really could do something for you. You . . . you were glad to see me. You said you were. . . . I thought we'd be friends again. I never thought about what I'd do if you really asked for my help. . . .

But, Helen, when I contacted you, I was asking you to do something legal—something you told me you'd done before. Isn't that right?

Yes, that's right.

And when you called me and told me you knew about an adoptable child, you told me the child's mother was dead and that the father either couldn't or didn't want to keep her—is that right?

Yes, I told you that. I must have been crazy. I can't sleep nights thinking about it. Where is she, Neely? Do you know? Maybe, if we can get her back and say it was all a mistake, maybe people will understand. No, no. No one will ever understand.

Neely listened to the recorded sound of her sobbing.

But when you brought the child to me, you gave me adoption release papers that seemed to be in order. You never said or did anything to suggest to me that you had obtained the child illegally. Is that correct?

Her voice was a groan. *I lied to you, Neely, and I'm so sorry. But I wanted to see you, to please you. Afterward, I put a message recorder on my phone so that if you called when I was at work, I wouldn't miss it.*

Again and again he had had her say it, coaxing her to say her full name and even her address and phone number so there could be no mistake as to her identity. She had done everything on her own. He was innocent—innocent.

Now Neely switched off the tape and stared out the window

of his condo, remembering that afternoon as if it had been a vivid but unbelievable dream.

He had reached behind a cot to turn off the tape recorder while Helen sobbed into her handkerchief. He'd resisted the urge to tell her she was an insane fool with as much appeal for him as a bag lady. Later, he was glad he'd resisted, because as things turned out, he had needed her.

He'd insisted she leave the boat alone and go and check into a nearby motel, afraid that if she returned to Los Angeles immediately, she might break down even further and go to the police. He'd gotten into his car then and driven up the coast, trying to think, trying to find a way out.

At first he considered going to Roger and telling him what he had done. The idea was terrifying, but Roger was the district attorney, and they had been friends for a long time. But the thought made him physically sick. He had to pull off the road to throw up.

Finally, he turned the car around and drove toward home. Pulling off the highway for gas, he had gotten out and paced as he waited for the attendant to fill the tank.

"D'you want a picture? A good picture by Shannon Buchanan. Just two dollars, mister."

He'd looked down at the little girl who tugged his pants leg. He'd looked at her once and then again, hardly believing what he saw. *A dead ringer*.

Slowly, he'd walked toward the young woman who waved to him from behind her easel. "May I draw your picture, sir?" she asked, smiling as he approached.

Nodding slightly, he'd sat down in the chair she offered, but as she stared at him to get his likeness, he continued to stare at the child. The idea, when it came, would have seemed too remote and impossible if he hadn't been so desperate.

As she finished the picture, he'd flashed his warmest smile. "My name is James Johnson. What's your name and where do you live?"

He had talked to her for a long time, grabbing at the essentials—no address, a transient, apparently without family or friends. *My God, there was a chance, a real chance, he could pull it off.*

After arranging to meet the young woman the next day, he had returned to Helen. He'd soothed her, said sweet things to her, and promised her that everything was going to be all right. The child was in a good home—the father loved her desperately. Neely would see to everything—she didn't need to worry—but was there any chance she would be able to help him forge and file a death certificate?

Helen had promised to do whatever he wanted—and she had. He had called Roger to explain he would be in Los Angeles for a couple of days and had driven Helen down, afraid to be seen on a plane with her.

She'd been frightened but, at his insistence, she had filed the death certificate exactly as he told her to. Afterward, he'd had no use for her. He had thought of her as garbage to be discarded.

But now her picture in the newspaper seemed to stare at him. He thought carefully—was there anything that could link her to him?

The tape, of course. It had been his protection, but now it was a bond to Helen—a threat. He cut it up in small pieces, and after he disposed of it, he went back into the kitchen. He righted the glass and sponged up the spilled gin and tonic. Then he mixed himself a double martini.

❧ 23 ❧

Phil had half an hour to kill before his flight left for Los Angeles on Tuesday. He went to the coffee shop and sat in the same booth where he had sat with Shannon and Mandy the previous evening.

He had almost laughed when he saw Shannon getting off the plane. He had asked her to keep a low profile, fearing she or Mandy might be recognized from their newspaper photographs, but he was unprepared for the long, loose dress she'd belted around her small frame and the scarves and sunglasses both she and Mandy wore.

"That is you, underneath that get-up, isn't it, Mrs. Valentine?" Phil had whispered, sidling up beside her and twirling an imaginary mustache while she searched the crowd looking for him.

Shannon had jumped. "Oh, Phil, you startled me. Yes, of course it's me. I borrowed this dress from Patty Marsh. Did you know she's lost thirty pounds?"

Mandy was tired, but she said she was hungry, and against his better judgment, Phil took them into the coffee shop. Mandy pouted when she learned there was no chocolate mousse pie on the menu, but she settled for an ice-cream sundae before they took off for the cabin.

It was, as Roger Connelly had said, a forty-five-minute drive into the mountains—a winding but well-paved road. It had been years since Phil had driven that route, but he found the cabin without much trouble.

In the dark it looked lonely and desolate, but Phil went in first to turn on the lights. Then he went back to the Jeep and, taking the sleeping Mandy from her arms, led Shannon inside.

"Are you sure you'll be all right here?" Phil asked, as Shannon peered into cupboards and closets and walked through every room. "It won't be for long and—"

"We'll be fine," Shannon said, facing him squarely, her jaw thrust forward in determination. "Mandy and I can do anything you need us to do if it will help you to find Patty's little girl."

Phil got a kick out of her independence and he knew she meant every word she said. It troubled him a little, though—her unshakable confidence that he was going to recover the Marsh child—but this was not the time to share his doubts with her. He helped her unload a sack of groceries. Then he lit the pilot lights in the heater and water heater before he said good night.

He had felt uneasy, leaving them there, and for a moment he'd almost changed his mind and taken them home to Salinas. But he'd known he was going to L.A. in the morning, and at the cabin, as Roger had pointed out, there was little chance they'd be discovered.

He thought about them now as he finished the last of his coffee and waited for his flight to be called. They were all alone up there, but he knew Shannon would be able to manage.

The loudspeaker came on and his flight was announced. Picking up his briefcase, he headed for the gate.

The yellow-gray smog layer that hovered over LAX seemed thicker than it had only a few days earlier, and when he left the artificial coolness of the terminal, the air that blasted his face was hot. Hailing a cab, he gave the address of Rossiter Division, LAPD.

He had the search warrant and the letter from Roger in his pocket and, though it was merely a courtesy, he would enlist the assistance of the Los Angeles police when he searched Helen Hanson's apartment.

Detective Stephanie Wilde, assigned to accompany him to Helen

Hanson's Silverlake district apartment, was a cheerful and pleasant woman about his own age, he guessed.

"What is it, exactly, you're looking for?" she asked, exiting the Hollywood Freeway and expertly negotiating the narrow, winding streets.

"I wish I knew," Phil told her honestly. "I'm hoping to find a link between the Hanson woman and a man by the name of Neely Smith. It would be very helpful to find his clothes in her closet or his shoes under the bed, but I guess that's too much to hope for."

Stephanie Wilde laughed. "At least you're able to search everything, every drawer and nook and cranny. If you were looking for a stolen TV or refrigerator, we'd have to limit your search to big objects."

She led him up a flight of stone steps to an old but graceful stucco apartment building and unlocked the door to a rear apartment lacking in natural light.

"We're keeping the place sealed pending the outcome of the murder investigation," Wilde told him, opening the venetian blinds. "Do you want help or would you rather I left you alone? Either way's fine with me."

"Suit yourself," Phil answered, walking slowly from room to room, looking for a sense of Helen Hanson.

The dead woman had been neat, he realized, noting the careful way her cosmetics were lined up on the dresser and the absence of clutter or strewn clothing. But, he decided, standing in the middle of the bedroom, that might only make his job harder.

There were no men's clothes in Helen's closets, no after-shave or extra toothbrushes in the small but tidy bathroom. Phil was not surprised. He had known from Robb Simpson's report that Helen Hanson had been a loner.

Panty hose, slips, pajamas, and underthings were neatly rolled in dresser drawers, but there were no letters, no pressed flowers, no personal little mementos that most women keep in drawers.

Satisfied he'd seen everything in the bedroom, he moved into the living room. Stephanie Wilde sat on a plaid sofa, flipping through a magazine. "Anything?"

"Not yet. Not in the bedroom, anyway." He walked toward a small desk in one corner of the room. The desktop held an assortment of pens and pencils, a blank memo pad, and a daily calendar turned to a date some weeks prior to when Hanson's body had washed up in the Bay.

The only notations made on pages dated the preceding two weeks were for a dental appointment early in June and an appointment with "James," followed by a telephone number. Phil stared at the number, thinking it was too good to be true. It was. He dialed the number and a voice answered, "Francois' Beauty Salon."

He asked to speak to James, and a moment later a high-pitched male voice came on the line. Phil asked whether Helen Hanson had been a regular patron, whether she had kept her last appointment.

"Oh, yes," James told him. "She wasn't a regular, but I remember doing her. She was so excited about having a new look for some trip up to the Bay."

"James, Helen Hanson was murdered in the Bay Area, and I'm investigating the case. It might be a big help to us if you could remember whether she mentioned somebody in particular who she was going to see—"

"Murdered! A lady of mine! Oh, how shocking! And I did such a good job on her hair—long and loose she wanted it, I remember that."

"I'm sure it looked good," Phil said, hardly believing the conversation, "but think hard. Did she say who she was going to meet—or why?"

"I just can't help you with that. I do so many—booked solid every day. Oh, dear!"

"Well, if you think of anything, call the Rossiter police station and leave a message for Phil Tewkes." Phil thanked him for his help and hung up.

He opened his notebook. She'd had her hair done special for a trip to the Bay. She almost certainly had expected to see Neely. It wasn't enough, but it was something. Phil scribbled the date of the appointment, weighing the probability that Helen Hanson had died within the next twenty-four hours—a time that meshed with the coroner's findings.

Phil continued his search of Hanson's desk. A ceramic soap dish held a few stamps, a roll of Scotch tape, paper clips, and one half of a broken locket containing a yellowed photo of a collie.

Utility bills and receipts going back several years were filed neatly in the desk drawers along with copies of tax forms and job evaluations citing Hanson as a punctual and conscientious employee.

Phil was struck again by the absence of anything personal or sentimental.

"What about books?" Stephanie Wilde suggested, standing before a mahogany-veneered bookcase in one corner of the living room.

"Why not?" Phil shrugged, kneeling in front of it to get a better look at the titles.

Hanson seemed to have leaned toward the classics, he noted, flipping through several volumes of Dickens, Shakespeare, and Robert Browning.

Stacked neatly on the bottom shelf were several high school yearbooks. *The Blue and Gold* meant nothing to Phil, but his pulse quickened when he read on the flyleaf, "Roosevelt High School, 1968."

Hadn't Smith graduated from Roosevelt? Phil thought back to the bio Terry had given him as he flipped through the pages of the book. He found Hanson's senior class photo showing a plain, solemn-faced girl with her hair pulled back in a ponytail.

Quickly, he scanned the alphabetical listings for Neely Smith, but he did not find him among the senior class or among the underclassmen.

Phil had risen, intending to call Roosevelt High to see if he could find out when Smith had graduated, when he realized the next book in the stack was the 1967 yearbook.

Opening it, he flipped to the senior photos, and a smiling, confident face stared up at him. Arlington Cornelius Smith. A red heart had been drawn around it, the only mark in any of Helen Hanson's books.

The simplicity of it, the ease with which the connection had been found, numbed Phil for a moment. Granted, the association went back twenty years, but they had known each other once—and whether the feeling had been mutual or not, Hanson had loved Neely Smith.

He passed the volume to Stephanie Wilde, who grinned widely.

"*Voilà!* It's a start," she said. "Not as good as his shoes under her bed, but now you know she knew him."

Encouraged, Phil picked up the stack of yearbooks, 1965–68, then saw there was a fifth, a thicker volume bound in orange. The *Princeton Bric-A-Brac, 1971.*

Wondering whether Princeton had been coed in 1971, Phil opened the front cover. Several carefully folded and yellowing pages of newsprint fluttered to the carpet in front of him.

The newspaper stories, mostly culled from the *Princeton Alumni Weekly*, spanned a period of some years, tracing Smith's career from Princeton to New York and back to California. The last was a notice that Smith had set up a practice in Los Angeles.

Phil studied the notices one at a time and handed them to Stephanie. When he finished the last one, he whistled softly. "Can you beat that? Can you imagine the lengths she must have gone to just to get copies of the *Alumni Weekly?*"

Stephanie nodded. "She must have been crazy about him. All those years—but it must have been one-sided."

"How do you know that?"

"Woman's intuition." Stephanie smiled. "No, seriously," she added, "you can bet if he'd ever sent her so much as a postcard, she'd have had it carefully boxed someplace where we would have found it."

Phil grinned. "Lady cops. Guess they aren't all that bad." He ducked away from Stephanie's feigned left hook. He hadn't felt this good in weeks.

Then he sobered, thinking of the dead woman, feeling something akin to pity—despite the fact that he was convinced it was Hanson who had abducted Suzanne Marsh. Helen Hanson had loved Smith, obsessively, it seemed. What she had done, Phil was willing to bet, she had done out of love for Smith. Would she have played so willingly into his hands, he wondered, if she had known Smith had once been implicated in a murder?

Phil thought back to everything Roger Connelly had told him about the girl who'd been murdered at Princeton. Roger thought the murder had never been solved. Officially, perhaps, it hadn't been. But Phil grimaced, certain now that Hanson had been Smith's second victim.

❧ 24 ❧

PHIL WANTED TO STRETCH, to walk around, but the seat-belt light was on due to turbulence. He was sure now that Neely Smith had murdered at least once—and probably twice. Connelly had said the girl at Princeton had been bludgeoned with a rock; Helen Hanson's skull had been crushed before she was dumped in the water. He was ready to bet that when he checked with the New Jersey police to get the details of the Princeton case, he'd find other similarities between the two deaths.

He had no idea what Smith's motives had been in the Princeton case, but Smith had been involved with Helen Hanson in the kidnapping of Suzanne Marsh. He had tried to use Mandy to close the case and eliminate the possibility of his ever being caught.

Again, it infuriated—and amazed—Phil to think how close Smith had come to pulling it off.

After the jet touched down at Monterey airport, Phil bounded toward the parking lot. He stopped for only a moment to scan the rack of newspapers.

Suspected Kidnap Victim Returned
to Roadside Artist—Murder Victim
Linked to Case

The heading seemed to jump off the page. Snatching up a paper, Phil read:

> The child called Amanda Knight, who was once thought to be kidnap victim Suzanne Marsh, has been returned to Shannon Buchanan. Police now believe Buchanan is the child's mother, despite earlier reports of a death certificate. . . . Helen Hanson, a murder victim whose body washed ashore at Carmel Bay several days ago, is believed to have been involved in the Marsh kidnapping. . . .

Phil groaned aloud. "Damn whoever broke the story. Damn."

He stood transfixed, not realizing he was crushing the paper in his hands until a clerk said, "You gonna pay for that paper, mister?"

"Yeah, sure," Phil mumbled, digging into his pocket for change. He threw some coins on the counter and walked away, unsteady, like a landlubber riding high seas.

Phil had planned to check out everywhere Smith went—everyone he talked to—in the hope of finding a lead to the whereabouts of Suzanne Marsh, but now that seemed futile. Smith would be on the alert. He wouldn't do anything to give himself away. . . . He'd be running scared.

Running scared . . .

Phil winced, remembering that Roger Connelly had been convinced Smith would try to escape if he thought he was under suspicion—and Smith would certainly have to be worried now.

Realizing the news had leaked stunned Phil for a moment, but abruptly he was all concentration. Digging out some more change, he found a phone booth and called the station. He hoped Lawler was aware that the story was out and had slapped a tail on Smith.

But Lawler wasn't at the station—no surprise so late in the evening—and Phil couldn't reach him at home either. Well, Smith wasn't going to get away even if Phil had to tail the bastard himself.

Flipping through his notebook, he realized to his chagrin that he'd never written down Smith's address or telephone number. He was about to call the station again when he had another idea. *Theresa.*

He didn't have her phone number either, but it took only a minute to find her parents' listing in the directory. When he saw the number, it looked familiar—even after all these years.

"Mrs. Ames," he began when a woman answered the phone, "I don't know if you'll remember me, but I used to be a good friend of Theresa's. Phil Tewkes is the name. I'm calling on police business and—"

"Phil! Of course I remember you. A fine-looking young man with red hair. How are you?"

"Great, Mrs. Ames. And it's nice to talk to you—but this is an emergency. I need to talk to Theresa. Can you give me her telephone number?"

"Wait a minute, Phil."

He waited, expecting her to return with the number, but the next voice he heard was Theresa's.

"Phil," she said, her voice dripping with reproach, "the story you were going to give me an exclusive on broke this evening. Did you forget our agreement?"

"Theresa! Thank God you're there. Listen, I didn't know the newspaper had the story until a few minutes ago when I got off a plane here at Monterey airport. And I need your help again—quick. Can you get me Neely Smith's address and telephone number?"

There was a long pause, but when she spoke her voice was much sweeter. "Of course, Phil. Anything for an old friend."

He gave her the number of the pay phone.

"Wait right there," she insisted. "I'll call you back in just a few minutes. Wait there."

After hanging up, he paced in front of the telephone, showing his badge when a cigar-smoking man tried to push past him. "Sorry. I'm waiting for an urgent call on police business," Phil told him.

The man made a guttural sound, then moved down to the next phone. He made his call and walked away, and Phil was still waiting. Glancing at his watch at least every other minute, he wondered what was taking Theresa so long.

After a half hour went by, he decided he should have tried to get Smith's address from the station. Why had he called Theresa in the first place? He shook his head. Could he be just another version of Helen Hanson—carrying a torch years after the flame should have been extinguished?

Finally, as he reached for the phone to call the station, it rang. Theresa sounded breathless. "Phil, Neely Smith lives down at the marina at Monterey Bay. Got a pencil?"

She gave him the address and telephone number, and he shouted his thanks as he slammed down the phone. He wasn't going to call the station and ask for a stakeout. He'd handle it himself. He didn't think of himself as a hell-and-thunder cop, but he felt a surging hatred for Neely Smith. If ever he had wanted to make an arrest, this was the time.

Driving to Monterey Bay, he thought about Shannon and Mandy. "Thank God for Roger Connelly," he told himself. "At least they're safe up there, and I don't have to worry about them."

When he reached the cluster of pseudo-Cape Cod buildings where Smith's condo was located, it was 11:00 p.m. There was nothing going on; the area was quiet. Phil looked around for a likely place to find a phone. He wanted to call Smith—fake a wrong number—to make certain he was home, then sit on his doorstep until morning if he had to, to make sure the bastard didn't bolt. Instinct told Phil he didn't want to arrest Smith yet—not if there was a chance he might still lead him to Suzanne Marsh.

He parked the Jeep and peered through the mist, checking numbers until he picked out Smith's condo. So this was where the respected man lived, secure in elegant trappings, far removed from the Marshes' grief and Shannon's ordeal. But Smith wouldn't feel very secure now, Phil told himself, not after he'd found out Helen Hanson's murder had been linked to the Marsh case.

Phil decided to walk past the building, then head toward the marina to look for a phone, but his attention was diverted by a movement in the hedges surrounding Smith's condo. Alert, he moved forward, narrowing his eyes for a better view. The hedges moved again. Motionless, he waited. A shadowy figure was slinking alongside the building.

In a sudden movement, one hand on his gun, he stepped toward the hedges. "Stop," he said. "I'm a police officer. Whoever you are, step out where I can see you."

The silence was palpable for a brief moment. Then the figure emerged from the hedges. "Phil, oh God, Phil, is that you? Don't shoot!"

"Jesus Christ, Theresa, are you crazy? What are you doing?" He took her by the arm and pulled her toward the Jeep, away from the condo. "How did you get here from your mother's in just . . ." He'd started to say "in just a half hour," but he'd stopped, realizing she'd deliberately kept him waiting. She must have been halfway here before she stopped to phone him. "Why you little . . ."

Theresa looked defiant. "You wouldn't have waited for me. I was sure of that. Besides, you promised me a story, and I intend to get it."

"Hiding in the bushes? You're nuts!" Phil shook his head. "What do you think you are, some junior detective? You could blow the whole thing, don't you realize that—coming out here on your own?"

Theresa grumbled as he pushed her into the Jeep. "I wasn't going to do anything. I just wanted to be here to see what was happening. And I thought maybe I could be of some help—"

"So maybe you can be," he said, disgusted, but willing to make use of her as long as she was there. "Find the nearest phone. Then come back here and let me know where it is."

He watched her, a dark shadow moving toward the marina, and it was almost twenty minutes before she returned. "There's a pay telephone to the north side of the boathouse. I checked it. It's working."

He took her arm. "Let's make a run for it. I don't want to be gone more than a few minutes."

He'd already decided that Theresa would make the call. "Apologize for calling so late," he told her, "but say you've just been asked to do an in-depth interview with Connelly and you'd like to have an answer by sometime tomorrow."

She sniffed. "I can write my own copy on this one, Phil. You don't have to tell me what to say."

He held the receiver so they both could hear, and Smith answered on the first ring. "Hello."

Theresa went into a spiel, sounding very convincing.

When Phil heard Smith it wasn't for the first time. He caught the voice and knew he was listening to Jack Avery. "I'll get back to you tomorrow, Terry. First thing. Good-bye." Smith rushed her off the phone.

Hurrying back to the Jeep, Phil felt excited despite himself. *Smith was there, in the condo, and he wasn't going to get away.*

Terry seemed to recover her dignity. "See, I didn't do any harm by coming. In fact, I've been a help to you."

He glanced at her as they climbed into the Jeep. "You ought to be thrashed."

She laughed and her smile was smug as she handed him her cigarette lighter.

Still annoyed, he struck the light and held it for her. "Haven't you heard about women's lib?" he grumbled.

She leaned forward to light her cigarette, but suddenly she seemed intent on something. "Phil, look!" she gasped. "It's Smith, he just came out."

Phil turned. A slender man of medium height had emerged from Smith's condo. Pulling on a jacket over a sweatsuit, he glanced around quickly. His gaze seemed to rest on the Jeep for a second, then he turned and walked down the driveway. With another furtive glance around, he proceeded toward the marina.

It was late for an evening jog, Phil thought, and he was walking, not running.

Phil turned to Terry. "You stay here. I want to see what he's doing."

Terry put a hand on his arm. "No, I'm coming too. If you're going to arrest him, I want my camera crew—"

"Terry, you *are* nuts. This isn't a B movie. I just want to get a good look at him." He opened the door and hopped out gingerly. "I said stay here, and I mean it."

It had been a long time since Phil had done surveillance. He felt slow and inept. But he kept Smith in view, though he was moving rapidly and heading straight for the marina.

Phil stopped, watching from the side of the boathouse, as Smith stepped up on the pier and, glancing around one last time, disappeared onto a boat.

A boat! Smith had a boat! Phil realized another part of the puzzle had fallen into place. That's how Smith had taken Helen Hanson's body out to sea. He'd dropped it overboard, expecting —Phil was certain—that it wouldn't be recovered until it was too decomposed for identification.

He felt his pulse beat fast in his ears as he moved forward, staying out of sight, to get a look at the name of the boat: *Lorelei II.*

He heard a hiss. "Phil."

Phil whirled around. "I told you to stay in the Jeep!"

Terry's eyes were wide with excitement. "Phil, that's Connelly's boat! What is he doing on Roger Connelly's boat at this hour of the night?"

"Connelly's boat? You're sure of it?"

"Of course I'm sure. His wife's name is Lorelei. The boat's named after her."

Suddenly, Phil felt as if he were riding in the eye of a tornado. *The district attorney's boat. Had Smith had the gall to murder Helen Hanson on the district attorney's boat?*

Theresa tugged his arm. "Tell me what you're thinking. I can tell just by looking at you that—"

"Hush a minute, will you? Give me time to think."

"But are you going to arrest him, Phil? You promised me a story, and I want my camera crew—"

"No, I'm not going to arrest him."

"Phil!" Her voice was a squeal. "Was it Smith who murdered Hanson on Connelly's boat and dumped her overboard?"

Once again he was astounded by her quickness of mind. Maybe, instead of chasing her home, he should level with her and put her wits to work.

He wheeled at the roar of a motor coming to life. The *Lorelei II* had loosed her moorings and was inching away from the pier.

They watched her slip into the darkness until she was out of sight.

"Now what?" Theresa whispered.

Phil shook his head. "I'm going to wait until that boat comes back, but there's no point waiting in the cold. I'll go get the Jeep." He hesitated. "You can stay if you want to."

He drove the Jeep to a spot where he had a view of the slip where the *Lorelei II* had been docked. Theresa needed no invitation to jump in beside him. She was shivering from the cold, damp air.

"Phil, what do you suppose he's doing out there?"

"Thinking, maybe. I don't know. He's got to be unnerved."

"Then there *is* a link. He *did* kill her! Phil, why didn't you tell me?"

He sighed. "Theresa, I'm telling you now. If you shut up for a minute, I'll tell you the rest of it."

"I'm sorry," she murmured, settling back.

"Helen Hanson kidnapped Suzanne Marsh. I'm sure of it. The kidnapper had a speech defect that Patty Marsh described in detail. Hanson had a speech defect that matched it. Even more important, the death certificate filed for Amanda Knight was included in a batch from the hospital where Hanson worked."

"And you think Hanson gave the child to Smith to sell or put up for adoption?"

"Yes." He opened the window of the Jeep a crack and turned on the motor to run the heater. "And my hunch is that when the posters of the missing Marsh child were plastered all over, Hanson panicked—and Smith had to shut her up."

"So he killed Helen and found a look-alike—Amanda Knight —to stand in for Suzanne Marsh." Theresa's voice was cool, as if she were delivering a newscast.

"He thought he had a pigeon in Shannon Buchanan, a transient who he was pretty sure wouldn't be able to prove the child was hers. Especially after he had Hanson plant a death certificate."

"Neely Smith! Phil, it sounds convincing, but, my God—he's a reputable attorney."

"That may be, but there's a case he was linked to when he was a student at Princeton. A girl was found dead—her head crushed just like the Hanson woman's. The last people to see her alive said she was with Smith. No charges were filed against him, but the murder was never solved."

Theresa leaned her head back against the seat. "What a story that's going to make! The DA's friend—his political advisor . . ."

"Connelly *is* his friend, all right," Phil said wryly. "That's what makes this so difficult." Phil stopped, deciding he shouldn't tell her the rest of it.

Theresa was silent. Phil looked at his watch. Smith had been gone over an hour.

"Suzanne Marsh," Theresa mused. "You really believe she's alive?"

Phil nodded. "If she were dead, there would have been no reason for Smith to concoct his elaborate cover-up."

Theresa seemed satisfied. She rested her head back while Phil stared toward the dark horizon. What would he do when the boat came back? He pondered the question in silence.

He thought Theresa was asleep when, an hour later, he glimpsed the lights of a boat. But she sat up, alert, as the drone of an engine signaled its return to shore.

Phil pushed her down lower in her seat and lowered himself until he could barely see above the dashboard.

It was the *Lorelei II* gliding effortlessly into her slip. A figure jumped ashore and tied her up, then hunched deeply into a windbreaker and moved swiftly down the dock.

Phil was uncertain what it was about Smith that looked different. He inched upward to get a better look. Theresa gasped and grabbed Phil's arm as the man strode past their line of sight.

"Phil! That's not Neely Smith—that's Roger Connelly."

Phil blinked to get a clearer focus. She was right . . . it *was*

Roger Connelly. For a moment he was stunned. Smith must have gone to meet Connelly. Theresa said it before he could:

"So that's what Smith was up to. A meeting with Connelly."

They watched, intent, as Roger Connelly got into an old, battered car in a parking area just north of the pier.

Phil looked back toward the dock, expecting to see Smith at any moment. But Connelly drove away, and the minutes ticked by with no sign of Neely Smith.

"Phil, what do you think the meeting was about? Do you think Smith opened up to him?"

"I don't know. Maybe." *Would Roger Connelly protect his friend a second time?*

"What do you think Connelly would do if he knew the truth about Smith? Surely, he wouldn't—couldn't—protect him."

"Don't be too sure about that."

"What do you mean? Is there something you haven't told me?"

Phil looked again toward the *Lorelei II*. Still no sign of Smith.

"Phil." Theresa's voice was insistent.

"When that girl was murdered at Princeton," Phil said, with a strange feeling of unease, "Connelly was part of Smith's alibi. He and a couple of other fraternity brothers swore Smith was in the fraternity house all night the night of the murder."

"Maybe he was . . ." she began.

Maybe he was. Oh, God, Phil realized. *Maybe he was.* Maybe Smith had not killed that girl. But someone—someone had. . . .

In an instant Phil had grabbed a flashlight and was out of the Jeep, running toward the *Lorelei II*. He jumped aboard, shining the light in all directions. "Smith! Police! Can you hear me?"

He heard the clatter of Theresa's heels as she jumped aboard behind him. He felt a growing dread—even before they started searching—that Smith was no longer on board.

"Maybe Connelly put him ashore," Theresa said, after they had searched the galley.

"Or in the water," Phil said.

❧ 25 ❧

ROGER CONNELLY was breathing hard as he drove his housekeeper's car away from the marina. Despite the chill of the night air, he could feel rivulets of perspiration running down his back.

The image of Neely's terror-stricken face swam before Roger in the glow of the headlights: Neely, who had very nearly torn apart the fabric of Roger's life, appealing for mercy as the first blow sent him reeling to his knees.

Roger had waited for Neely below deck—just as he'd waited once before. But this time he had not been hasty.

"Roger?" Neely had called to him as he boarded the *Lorelei II.* "Are you on board?"

"Yes, Neely, come on down."

Even in the dim light of the cabin, Neely looked frightened, but he struggled with a smile when he looked at Roger. "What's up? Ever since I got your call I—"

"Untie the boat, Neely. Let's take her out."

"At this time of night? Roger, I don't—"

"Untie the boat."

Neely did as he was told, then followed Roger's command to steer the boat toward open water.

Roger stood behind Neely at the wheel. "Is this how you did it, Neely?" His voice was soft. "Is this how you killed Helen Hanson?"

Neely whirled. "What are you talking about? I didn't kill her."

A harsh laugh escaped from Roger's throat. "What? You didn't kill Helen Hanson? That's odd. The sheriff thinks you did."

Confusion twisted Neely's face. "God, Roger, I swear I didn't kill her. I hardly knew her."

Roger waved his hand. "I know that. You said it over and over again on the tape."

Neely blanched.

"You didn't know I listened to the tape, did you, Neely? I guess I forgot to tell you. I was in your condo—remember when I arranged to have you go to Los Angeles for a few days to handle some business for me? Well, I had other business to attend to. I needed to find a letter."

"Letter? What letter?"

"You remember the letter, Neely. The one—what was her name?—Kolanchuk had you give to me the night she was murdered back at Princeton. The letter begging me to meet her that night—and threatening me with a lawsuit if I didn't. All these years—I was never certain you'd destroyed it."

"Roger, that's crazy. Of course I destroyed it. . . . Why would you worry about it now?"

Roger shrugged. "The governor's mansion is in sight. I couldn't run the risk of having that letter fall into the wrong hands."

"Roger, I destroyed the letter the same day I swore to the police that we were both in our room all night. Anyway, all you had to do was ask me. You didn't have to go looking for it."

"I thought you might have saved it for a rainy day—and, Neely, it's raining for you now. You're about to be named an accessory to kidnapping and, unless I miss my guess, for the murder of Helen Hanson."

Neely's eyes grew wide.

"You didn't know I knew about the two of you, Neely, but I knew, all right. The tape told me everything."

Neely slumped over, his hand on his stomach, as if he were going to throw up.

"I didn't find the letter, but I found the tape hidden behind a picture. Can't say I admire your taste in art, but I had to find out why the tape was so valuable that you had hidden it so carefully."

Roger's voice remained steady, but he felt his control dissolving into rage. "I listened to it twice, and then I put it back, just the way I'd found it."

Neely struggled to speak. "Roger, if you listened to the tape, you know—you've got to believe—I didn't do it knowingly. And no matter what you think about my involvement with Helen, I swear . . . I swear I didn't kill her."

"Don't worry, pal—we are pals, aren't we?—I'll protect you again—just as I protected you back at Princeton. Your alibi wouldn't have stood up then without my backing you up."

Neely groaned. "Roger, I was *your* alibi! I *was* in our room. It was you. You were out that night. You swore you were with me so that I would be *your* alibi."

Roger heard the sound of his own laughter. "A detail," he said. "Kolanchuk was nothing, a nobody. Claimed she was pregnant with my child. *My child*, when we all knew she slept with half the guys on campus."

Roger paused, reliving the rage he'd felt then. "I hit her just to shut her mouth. She fell and hit her head. She was bleeding badly. I started to help her, but then I realized I couldn't let her live. Roger Connelly had too great a future ahead of him to let himself be ruined by a charge of assault and battery. I couldn't let her drag me down. I couldn't let Hanson drag me down either. I would have looked like a pathetic fool."

Neely's eyes glazed with horror. "My God, Roger—*you* killed Helen."

"I had to do it, Neely. I had to. She was hysterical. She would have gone to the police."

"Roger, I'm sorry. God, I risked everything to try to make it right. Until a few hours ago, I thought I had."

Roger continued, ignoring Neely's pleading. "And I knew how I would kill her. The second time I listened to the tape I heard the gulls in the background. I knew you and Hanson had been here, on *my* boat. It was easy for me to get her back here. I just called and told her you had sent for her."

Neely licked his lips. "All right. You killed Helen. But no one will suspect you. Believe me, Roger, no one will suspect the DA. I'll help you like I helped you before—like I've always helped you."

"I don't need your help, Neely, because you're right. The authorities will never suspect me. It's *you* they suspect. I told Tewkes about Kolanchuk. They'd have dug it up anyway when they investigated your background, and I deliberately incriminated you —once and for all."

"Roger, Roger—you know I didn't do it."

Roger only smiled. "But Tewkes thinks you did, and he's already tied you to Hanson's murder. You'd be under surveillance this very minute if I hadn't warned them not to put a tail on you."

As Roger spoke he moved toward the bar, casually, as if he were going to mix a drink. But he felt strength in every cell of his body. Neely would pay for what he had done to him.

"They'll never find you, Neely. They'll think you took off because you knew they were closing in—which is precisely why I made certain the whole story got leaked to the press."

Moving slowly, he picked up the pipe he had positioned behind the bar. He could smell Neely's fear. "They'll never find you. I'll see to that."

He whirled and, before Neely could defend himself, delivered the first, crushing blow.

Again, he told himself, venting his rage, he had done what he had to do.

"Don't touch that!" Phil's voice rang out as Theresa moved toward the bar of the *Lorelei II*.

Theresa turned to look at him. "Why?"

"We saw Smith come aboard. He isn't here now. For all we know, he may be out in the water. If this is a crime scene, we mustn't touch anything or we run the risk of destroying useful prints."

"Crime scene? Phil, you don't seriously believe that Roger Connelly killed Neely Smith?"

He sniffed, detecting something, then bent on one knee and ran his fingers lightly against the galley planks. "I don't know, but this is moist. It's just been swabbed down." He smelled his fingers. "Ammonia."

He followed the path of moistness out to the deck and examined the area by flashlight. If Connelly had murdered Smith, he would have had to drag the body across the deck in order to dump it overboard.

Phil didn't find anything, but he was pretty sure the lab boys would discover traces of blood—maybe hair and skin samples. Straightening, he took one last look around. "Let's get back on shore. We need help."

They hurried down the pier and climbed into the Jeep.

"What are you going to do?" Theresa asked.

"If Smith doesn't turn up, we'll want the boat impounded and thoroughly searched—but that'll have to wait until morning."

Phil slumped against the wheel, absorbing the strange twist of events. He had been sure—convinced—that Neely Smith was the key to the kidnapped Marsh child and the murder of Helen Hanson. But if Smith had been murdered, Phil was now looking for a third person. As bizarre as it seemed, he suspected the district attorney of Monterey County. Could the man who held that office be a killer?

That girl at Princeton. Was it possible Smith had covered for Connelly, not the other way around? And Hanson. Could Connelly have murdered her? Why? And why Neely Smith? He had thought he understood Neely Smith's involvement with Hanson, but how did Connelly fit in?

Hanson had kidnapped Suzanne Marsh. That much Phil was sure of. And she'd been murdered, he was still certain, in an effort to protect the stolen child's whereabouts. If Connelly had killed Hanson, and then killed Smith, was he somehow involved with the kidnap? Was Connelly trying to eliminate everyone who could possibly tie him to the case?

It seemed outrageous. Phil groaned aloud. If he was right, the DA had to be insane. Who would believe that? Could he believe it himself? And where the hell did it end? If Connelly was insane enough to kill three times, who else might he feel was a threat?

He tensed. Shannon! Shannon was ensconced in the Connelly's cabin, ready to identify Neely Smith! *In the DA's cabin, at the DA's request.*

Theresa's question brought it home. "Where do you suppose Connelly is now?"

"That's what worries me." He turned the key. The Jeep roared to life in the darkness.

"Why would Connelly be involved with this?" Theresa echoed the question that badgered Phil as he shifted into gear and drove off. "Phil, he's rich, he's powerful, he's got a great future ahead of him."

Phil remembered the girl at Princeton. *But maybe an untidy past.* There was no time to alert the station. He had to get to Shannon.

❧ 26 ❧

PHIL DROVE with his foot to the floor, the Jeep careening around curves and bouncing sharply up the mountain roads.

"Where are we going?"

Intent on the road, Phil ignored Theresa's question until she repeated it.

"Phil, dammit, what's wrong? You're driving like a madman."

"Shannon and her daughter are in Connelly's cabin." The words seared Phil's throat.

"For God's sake, what are they doing there?"

He blinked to keep the road in focus. "Because I'm a damn fool."

Theresa started to say something, broke off, and didn't say another word.

Soon they rose above the fog that hovered near the coast. The air was clear, and finally the peak of the Connelly cabin loomed solitary in the moonlight.

"It looks peaceful," she said.

Peaceful. Phil gritted his teeth. Connelly had had at least an hour's start on them while he and Theresa had searched the boat. Connelly could have been there, bludgeoned Shannon and Mandy, and been long gone by now.

Theresa was talking again, but Phil hardly heard. He berated himself for ever having laid his cards on the table for anyone but Lawler. The knowledge that he had inadvertently tipped Connelly, possibly prodding him to further violence, snaked icily down Phil's spine.

God, he prayed, though the word did not come naturally to his lips, *let them be alive, let them be safe.*

It seemed ominously quiet as the Jeep crunched up the graveled driveway to the cabin. Not even a light was on. Phil reminded himself that it was, after all, 4:00 a.m., but still—not even a night-light?

He was out of the Jeep before the engine died. Running up the small incline, he made a fist to pound on the door, then thought better of it. Connelly might still be inside. He tested the door gently. It swung open at his touch.

"Shannon . . ." His voice was barely a whisper. His heart pounded. *She wasn't going to answer.*

He fumbled for a light switch, found one, finally, on the wall beside the door. He held his breath as light filled the room.

The living room was tidy, nothing seemed out of place. Several charcoal drawings lay on the coffee table. Cautiously, he moved toward the bedrooms, but his feet were leaden. He could hardly move. *Shannon, Shannon, what did I do to you?*

He froze as a muffled sound came from the bedroom. Waiting, he saw a shadow in the doorway.

"Oh, Phil, it's you. Thank God." Shannon was holding a lamp in both hands, upraised, as if it were a weapon. The cord trailed ridiculously behind her.

Relief flooded through him. He took the lamp out of her hands. "Just what would you have done with that?"

She smiled sheepishly, color flooding her cheeks. She looked so forlorn, so frightened. He put his arms around her, held her close. "You're okay, Shannon, nothing can happen to you." He stood, holding her, smelling the sweet fragrance of her hair. "I won't let anything happen to you."

"Oh!" Theresa stood in the doorway. "Oh, Phil, she's all right!"

She sounded almost disappointed, Phil thought. Did she mind finding Shannon in his arms or simply finding her alive? A corpse would have made a better story. In his euphoria, he let it pass.

Exhausted, he fell heavily onto the sofa, resting his head against the back. He closed his eyes for just a moment. He hadn't slept for twenty-four hours and these last minutes had drained him.

"Phil." Shannon's voice was soft. "Would you like a cup of coffee?" She turned to Theresa. "Would you like some too—uh, Mrs. Tewkes?"

Phil struggled to open his eyes. "Shannon, this is Terry Ames. She's not Mrs. Tewkes—she's a nosy newscaster who stashed herself in my Jeep."

"Phil!" Theresa bristled. "What a thing to say."

Grinning, Phil closed his eyes again.

"Is there a Mrs. Tewkes?" Shannon asked shyly, after a moment of silence.

He had to open his eyes again. He looked straight at her. "No, there's no Mrs. Tewkes."

Shannon smiled. "I'm happy to meet you, Miss Ames." She headed toward the kitchen.

"Shannon!" The little girl's sleepy voice stirred Phil. Mandy was standing in the middle of the room, looking from him to Theresa. Her jaw was thrust forward—just like her mother's. "Where's my Shannon?" she demanded.

"Mommy. I'm your Mommy. And I'm right here, Mandy." Shannon hurried from the kitchen. "Look, Mandy, we have company. You remember Mr. Tewkes. And this is his friend—"

Before Shannon could finish, Theresa gasped. "This is Mandy Knight?"

The child hid her face in Shannon's battered, chenille robe.

In one swoop Theresa knelt beside her. She took the child's chin in her hand, turning her face toward the light. "Dear God," she said, turning to stare at Phil. "I know where Suzanne Marsh is."

For a moment the only sound was the faint perk of the coffeepot. Phil stood, his exhaustion forgotten.

"Patty's little girl? Miss Ames, do you really?" Shannon's voice rang with joy.

Phil spoke sharply. "What are you saying, Theresa?"

"I know where she is. I've seen pictures of Mandy. But, God, I didn't spot the resemblance—not until now when I actually saw this child. She is . . . she really is . . . a mirror image of Kelly Connelly."

Kelly Connelly. Phil went rigid. The daughter the Connellys had adopted last year. Phil had known about the adoption, but he had never seen the child. Now it all fell into place. He knew where Connelly fit in. Hanson and Smith had placed the kidnapped Marsh child with Roger Connelly and his wife. Connelly couldn't have known the child's origin then, but he certainly knew it now. He had murdered twice to hide the truth. His "daughter" was Suzanne Marsh.

The first rays of light shone through the window, brightening the paneled room. "Phil," Shannon pleaded, "if you know where Suzy is, can't we go and get her?"

"Not until I alert my camera crew. I want them at the Connellys' home."

Theresa kept talking, her voice a droning background to Phil's thoughts. Connelly hadn't needed to come after Shannon. A sinking terror washed over him. Of course not. Shannon wasn't the threat. Only the kidnapped child was. Suzanne—Kelly. Was Connelly insane enough to kill her?

He jerked the phone out of Theresa's hand. "I've got to call the station."

❧ 27 ❧

It was not quite dawn when Roger Connelly walked quietly into Kelly's pink and white room and stood at the end of her bed. He studied her in the soft glow of the night-light. She was the most precious thing in his life.

He remembered the rush of love he'd felt the first time he'd held her—the day Neely had brought her to them.

Lorelei had not wanted children, had never wanted them. Only his insistence that as a family man he would be more popular when he ran for public office persuaded her to change her mind. She would not consider carrying a child, but she did consent to adoption. And it had taken only a word to Neely for them to circumvent the red tape and long wait of adopting through an agency. Neely had found them the perfect child as easily as he might have found them a new investment.

But a new investment would have been legal.

Never, not for the briefest moment, had he ever questioned the story Neely told him. "Her mother is dead, and the father is willing to sign the papers. The child is yours."

And how quickly she had become theirs—or at least his. If Lorelei's response had been slow in coming, Roger had found it easy to lavish affection on the child from the first day.

He remembered the shock he'd felt when he'd first heard the tape—the wrench in his gut when he'd realized his little Kelly was the missing Suzanne Marsh.

He'd been staggered—dazed. If he could have, he would have killed Neely right then.

He looked at his beautiful Kelly again, a picture book child, with her blond curls and long lashes arcing over soft, pink cheeks. Tears ran down his own cheeks. She was so fragile, so soft, so utterly devoted to him.

It was going to be so hard to kill her.

It was a tight squeeze with four of them in the Jeep, but Theresa refused to be left behind, and Phil was not of a mind to leave Shannon and Mandy in Connelly's cabin alone.

He had called the station but said only that he suspected there might be trouble at the Connelly house, that he was proceeding there and wanted backup available on Route 1 at the junction to Seventeen Mile Drive, in case he should need it.

Phil was convinced now that Connelly had murdered both Helen Hanson and Neely Smith. But, by God, the man was still the district attorney. He couldn't send a fleet of sheriff's cars screeching up to his door.

If the child was all right—and he found himself praying to God that she was—he would question Connelly alone before doing anything else. But it was comforting to Phil to know that if he ran into trouble, his backup would not be far away.

Shannon had thrown on a pair of jeans and a shirt and now sat wedged between him and Theresa, holding Mandy. The tension in the car was tangible. No one—not even Theresa—spoke. Bright-eyed and wide awake, Mandy sat quietly too. Phil glanced at the child now and then, thinking of Suzanne Marsh, who now answered to Kelly.

He had been annoyed with Theresa for playing junior detective on this night that had begun so long ago. But now he was grateful she had witnessed the comings and goings on the Connelly boat with him—and indebted to her for adding the last piece to the puzzle.

The sun was up as they descended from the mountain road to the main highway that led to Seventeen Mile Drive. Phil signaled as he passed two sheriff's cars parked at a curve in the road and proceeded down the drive to the imposing grandeur of the Connelly estate.

Pine trees circled the house like sentinels. Sunlight shimmered through the lingering wisps of fog, reflecting on an expansive wall of glass. It was peaceful, beautiful. By daylight the convictions of the night seemed almost impossible to believe. Braking, Phil hesitated, but only a moment. Then he wheeled the Jeep in front of the house.

"You stay here," he ordered Theresa. He turned to Shannon. "You keep her here even if you have to hold her by the hair."

He wasn't hesitant now. He ran up the brick steps, rang the doorbell, and heard an elaborate set of chimes. Several minutes passed before the door was opened by a thin, older woman in a long, quilted robe.

"Investigator Phil Tewkes," he said, holding his identification toward her. "I'm with the sheriff's office. I have to talk to the district attorney immediately."

The woman stared at his identification for a moment. "I'm sorry, sir," she said. "The district attorney is not at home."

"Was he at home at all last night?"

"I'm the housekeeper. I'm sure I wouldn't know," the woman responded, looking at him askance. "But he was here earlier and decided to take his boat out. He said it was a perfect morning to watch the sun come up from out at sea."

And to make certain the boat was cleaned of any traces of Neely Smith. Damn, I should have had the boat impounded.

"How long ago did he leave?"

The woman was clearly hesitant and somewhat huffy now. "Sir," she began, "the district attorney will probably be in his office as usual sometime this morning. Perhaps it would be better if you contacted him there."

"Please, I need to know. What time did he leave?"

"At least an hour ago. I dressed his daughter and fed her breakfast. Then he took her—"

"He took the child? The child is with him?" Phil's voice rose in fear.

Turning, he ran back and jumped in the Jeep. "Connelly took Suzanne to the marina."

"Phil, he wouldn't . . . ?" Theresa started to ask.

"God knows what he'll do," he told her. "At this point, he can't be rational."

He tore down the road, honking as he approached his backup cars, signaling to them to follow him.

"I want a camera crew—"

"Dammit, Theresa! Don't you realize there's a life at stake here!"

It was an agonizingly long drive to the marina, and Phil broke every speed limit, the sirens in the backup cars behind them screaming a warning to the early morning traffic.

Mandy turned to look back at the flashing lights. "Shannon, don't take my Shannon!"

Shannon's voice was calm. "Mommy's fine, Mandy. This isn't like the other time. Mr. Tewkes is our friend."

From a rise, as they passed Neely Smith's condo, they could see the marina clearly, the line of tall, colorful masts and pennants whipping with the breeze.

Phil's gaze traveled the length of the dock closest to the boathouse where the *Lorelei II* had been docked. His brows knit in consternation as he realized the boat was still there—sleek and commanding, like Connelly himself. It was moored as it had been earlier.

Theresa saw it too. "Phil, the boat is there! Are you sure he was on his way here?"

Phil said nothing as the Jeep careened downhill and screeched to a stop at the edge of the pier, the sheriff's cars just behind him. Ordering his passengers to stay in the Jeep, he turned off the ignition. He started to bolt when a groan from Theresa made his blood run cold.

"Oh, God, there he is! Damn you, Phil, I don't have a crew—"

Roger Connelly jumped heavily onto the pier from the deck of the *Lorelei II*. His attention seemed focused on the blanket-wrapped bundle he carried.

Phil walked slowly toward Connelly. His heart froze in his chest. Connelly was dripping wet, and two little legs hung limply from the blanket.

Suzanne! Phil froze in his tracks. His gaze narrowed until all he could see were those two dangling legs. Dear God, oh, goddamn —he had drowned her.

Connelly seemed unaware of Phil. He crooned softly, staring down at the child. "It was just a game, Kelly. Daddy didn't mean it. I didn't mean to hurt you."

Shannon rushed past Phil, sobbing. She faced Connelly. "Give me Suzanne!" She beat at his arms. "You killed her! You killed Patty's little girl."

Connelly looked up. His expression was glazed, as if he had awakened from a dream.

Then Phil heard a beautiful sound. The child Connelly carried was crying.

Shannon yanked the sodden bundle from Connelly, who gave it up without a fight. He stood still, arms hanging at his sides. "I . . . I couldn't hurt her. I tried . . . but I couldn't . . ."

Shannon rocked the child in her arms. "Suzy, Suzy, you're all right." She looked at Phil, tears running down her cheeks. "I'm going to call Patty Marsh."

Phil blinked hard, then he led Connelly toward the waiting deputies.

Theresa ran to meet them. "Can you hold him a few minutes? I have a crew on the way."

He glared at her. "Sorry, Miss Ames. You'll have to do without your footage."

"Phil! Phil, can you come here?" Shannon called as she put Suzy in the Jeep.

Weary, he walked over and put his hand on her shoulder. She pointed to the two little girls.

Suzanne and Mandy were seated side by side, wide-eyed and solemn-faced. Except for the difference in their size and builds— Suzy Marsh was larger—the resemblance was truly remarkable.

Shannon took a corner of the blanket and used it to dry Suzy's hair, fluffing it and combing it with her fingers so that it curled in the same way as Mandy's. Twins, Phil marveled, shaking his head. They could almost pass for twins.

He walked back to where Connelly stood, slumped between the deputies.

"Tewkes, for Pete's sake," one of them said. "This is the district attorney!"

Phil looked at Connelly. "Sir," he began, "it is my duty to advise you of your rights."

❧ *Epilogue* ❧

TERRY AMES, on the screen, was more beautiful than ever. Excitement agreed with her, Phil thought. He knotted his tie, muttered darkly, undid it, and knotted it again.

Terry's dark eyes were aglow and her voice rang with conviction. "The Bay Area, the state, and the nation are still in shock over the arrest—witnessed by this reporter—of Monterey County District Attorney Roger Connelly in connection with at least two murders and one count of child endangerment."

Still unsatisfied, Phil undid the tie and walked to the bedroom to stand in front of the mirror and start the process again.

"The child known as Kelly Connelly," Terry went on, "who was placed with Connelly and his wife, Lorelei, last July, has been positively identified as Suzanne Marsh, abducted from a shopping center only days earlier.

"Sheriff's deputies in Monterey County believe Connelly was unaware of the child's origins when he and his wife adopted her— but that learning who she was prompted his alleged murder of the abductor, Helen Hanson, and her accomplice, Connelly's longtime friend and attorney-advisor, A. Cornelius Smith."

Phil walked back to the set and watched Terry for a minute.

"In view of the charges now levied against the district attorney, law enforcement officials are reviewing the details of an unsolved murder that occurred at Princeton University nearly twenty years ago when Roger Connelly was a student there. As for Suzanne Marsh . . ."

Pulling on his suit coat, Phil switched off the set with his knee.

As for Suzanne Marsh . . . He hadn't witnessed the reunion of Suzanne with her parents, but Shannon had. She had refused to be separated from the child until she had personally handed her to Patty Marsh.

"I was afraid Suzy might be strange with Patty," Shannon had told Phil later. "She'd been through so much and was so upset—but the moment she went into Patty's arms, she cuddled right against her. She knows Patty is her mother, Phil. I felt it."

Thinking of Shannon, he checked his watch. They had agreed to meet at one o'clock.

Late yesterday, after Connelly was in custody and Suzy was safe with the Marshes, he had checked Shannon and Mandy into a seaside inn just outside Carmel. She hadn't received the rest of their Texas inheritance yet, but it would be only a matter of days. Meantime, she was determined to find a place to live and to buy a new car. Phil had agreed to help her find the right car, and he'd told her he knew just the right house.

He took one last look around, wondering if he had time to tidy up the table where the half-finished model of the *Simón Bolívar* had lain untouched for so long. Moe screeched at him, demanding attention.

"Bird, there is virtue in patience."

He locked the door, realizing for the first time that it needed a new coat of paint. Backing the Jeep out of the driveway, he took a long view of the neighborhood. Not bad, he decided. Far from affluent, but the lawns were tidy, there was never much traffic, and children could play in the street. He waved jauntily to a neighbor who was washing his car, then he went to keep his appointment with Shannon.

In the parking lot, he pulled up alongside Shannon's car. She wasn't in it. She had gone on ahead to wait for him. Getting out of the Jeep, he straightened his tie again. Then, swinging his arms, he walked around to the front of the courthouse.

They were standing at the foot of the steps. Shannon wore a short, pink dress, crisp-looking, with a matching jacket, her legs shapely in white high-heeled shoes. Mandy was decked out in a frilly party dress in the identical shade of pink as her mother's. He couldn't decide which one was more adorable.

Mandy ran to him. "Hi, Mr. Toots!"

He scooped her up. "You're as pretty as a princess," he told her.

She giggled delightedly, but when Shannon looked up at him, her eyes were big and serious.

"Phil," she began, "there's something . . . something I have to tell you."

He took a tighter hold on Mandy, a wave of apprehension flooding through him. "Can't it wait until later?" he asked.

She hung her head. "No. I have to tell you now."

He steeled himself.

"Phil, do you remember when you insisted I tell you my real name?"

He nodded. "Sure, I remember. You told me your name was—"

"Ruth Ann Stone," she finished for him, tears springing to her eyes. "Well, I just remembered. It's not Ruth Ann Stone. I guess I made that name up. My real name is—"

He kissed her on the mouth before she could finish. He hugged both of them tight. Then, still carrying Mandy, he grasped Shannon's arm and led her up the steps to the license bureau.

Mandy was learning to call her Mommy. He would call her Mrs. Tewkes. It might sound a little old-fashioned, but, by God, it was a name he would be sure of.